A SENSE OF REALITY

Graham Greene was born in 1904. On coming down from Balliol College, Oxford, he worked for four years as sub-editor on *The Times*. He established his reputation with his fourth novel, *Stamboul Train*. In 1935 he made a journey across Liberia, described in *Journey Without Maps*, and on his return was appointed film critic of the *Spectator*. In 1926 he had been received into the Roman Catholic Church and visited Mexico in 1938 to report on the religious persecution there. As a result he wrote *The Lawless Roads* and, later, his famous novel *The Power and the Glory*. *Brighton Rock* was published in 1938 and in 1940 he became literary editor of the *Spectator*. The next year he undertook work for the Foreign Office and was stationed in Sierra Leone from 1941 to 1943. This later produced the novel, *The Heart of the Matter*, set in West Africa.

As well as his many novels, Graham Greene wrote several collections of short stories, four travel books, six plays, three books of autobiography – *A Sort of Life*, *Ways of Escape* and *A World of My Own* (published posthumously) – two of biography and four books for children. He also contributed hundreds of essays, and film and book reviews, some of which appear in the collections *Reflections* and *Mornings in the Dark*. Many of his novels and short stories have been filmed and *The Third Man* was written as a film treatment. Graham Greene was a member of the Order of Merit and a Companion of Honour.
Graham Greene died in April 1991.

ALSO BY GRAHAM GREENE

Graham Greene

A SENSE OF REALITY

VINTAGE

Published by Vintage 1999

2 4 6 8 10 9 7 5 3 1

First published in Great Britain by
The Bodley Head 1963
First published in paperback by
Penguin Books 1968

Vintage
Random House, 20 Vauxhall Bridge Road,
London SW1V 2SA

Random House Australia (Pty) Limited
20 Alfred Street, Milsons Point, Sydney
New South Wales 2061, Australia

Random House New Zealand Limited
18 Poland Road, Glenfield,
Auckland 10, New Zealand

Random House South Africa (Pty) Limited
Endulini, 5A Jubilee Road, Parktown 2193,
South Africa

Random House UK Limited Reg. No. 954009

A CIP catalogue record for this book
is available from the British Library

ISBN 0 09 928256 9

Papers used by Random House UK Ltd are natural,
recyclable products made from wood grown in sustain-
able forests. The manufacturing processes conform to the
environmental regulations of the country of origin

Printed and bound in Great Britain by
The Guernsey Press Co. Ltd., Guernsey, Channel Islands

TO

JOHN AND GILLIAN SUTRO

CONTENTS

UNDER THE GARDEN

PART ONE

1

IT was only when the doctor said to him, 'Of course the fact that you don't smoke is in your favour,' Wilditch realized what it was he had been trying to convey with such tact. Dr Cave had lined up along one wall a series of X-ray photographs, the whorls of which reminded the patient of those pictures of the earth's surface taken from a great height that he had pored over at one period during the war, trying to detect the tiny grey seed of a launching ramp.

Dr Cave had explained, 'I want you clearly to understand my problem.' It was very similar to an intelligence briefing of such 'top secret' importance that only one officer could be entrusted with the information. Wilditch felt gratified that the choice had fallen on him, and he tried to express his interest and enthusiasm, leaning forward and examining more closely than ever the photographs of his own interior.

'Beginning at this end,' Dr Cave said, 'let me see, April, May, June, three months ago, the scar left by the pneumonia is quite obvious. You can see it here.'

'Yes, sir,' Wilditch said absent-mindedly. Dr Cave gave him a puzzled look.

'Now if we leave out the intervening photographs for the moment and come straight to yesterday's, you will observe that this latest one is almost entirely clear, you can only just detect . . .'

'Good,' Wilditch said. The doctor's finger moved over what might have been tumuli or traces of prehistoric agriculture.

'But not entirely, I'm afraid. If you look now along the whole series you will notice how very slow the progress has been. Really by this stage the photographs should have shown no trace.'

'I'm sorry,' Wilditch said. A sense of guilt had taken the place of gratification.

9

'If we had looked at the last plate in isolation I would have said there was no cause for alarm.' The doctor tolled the last three words like a bell. Wilditch thought, Is he suggesting tuberculosis?

'It's only in relation to the others, the slowness . . . it suggests the possibility of an obstruction.'

'Obstruction?'

'The chances are that it's nothing, nothing at all. Only I wouldn't be *quite* happy if I let you go without a deep examination. Not *quite* happy.' Dr Cave left the photographs and sat down behind his desk. The long pause seemed to Wilditch like an appeal to his friendship.

'Of course,' he said, 'if it would make you happy . . .'

It was then the doctor used those revealing words, 'Of course the fact that you don't smoke is in your favour.'

'Oh.'

'I think we'll ask Sir Nigel Sampson to make the examination. In case there is something there, we couldn't have a better surgeon . . . for the operation.'

Wilditch came down from Wimpole Street into Cavendish Square looking for a taxi. It was one of those summer days which he never remembered in childhood: grey and dripping. Taxis drew up outside the tall liver-coloured buildings partitioned by dentists and were immediately caught by the commissionaires for the victims released. Gusts of wind barely warmed by July drove the rain aslant across the blank eastern gaze of Epstein's virgin and dripped down the body of her fabulous son. 'But it hurt,' the child's voice said behind him. 'You make a fuss about nothing,' a mother – or a governess – replied.

2

This could not have been said of the examination Wilditch endured a week later, but he made no fuss at all, which perhaps aggravated his case in the eyes of the doctors who took his calm for lack of vitality. For the unprofessional to enter a hospital or to enter the services has very much the same effect; there is a sense of relief and indifference; one is placed quite helplessly on a conveyor-belt with no responsibility any more for anything. Wilditch felt himself protected by an organization, while the English summer dripped outside on the coupés of the parked cars. He had not felt such freedom since the war ended.

The examination was over – a bronchoscopy; and there remained a nightmare memory, which survived through the cloud of the anaesthetic, of a great truncheon forced down his throat into the chest and then slowly withdrawn; he woke next morning bruised and raw so that even the act of excretion was a pain. But that, the nurse told him, would pass in one day or two; now he could dress and go home. He was disappointed at the abruptness with which they were thrusting him off the belt into the world of choice again.

'Was everything satisfactory?' he asked, and saw from the nurse's expression that he had shown indecent curiosity.

'I couldn't say, I'm sure,' the nurse said. 'Sir Nigel will look in, in his own good time.'

Wilditch was sitting on the end of the bed tying his tie when Sir Nigel Sampson entered. It was the first time Wilditch had been conscious of seeing him: before he had been a voice addressing him politely out of sight as the anaesthetic took over. It was the beginning of the week-end and Sir Nigel was dressed for the country in an old tweed jacket. He had tousled white hair and he looked at Wilditch with a far-away attention as though he were a float bobbing in midstream.

'Ah, feeling better,' Sir Nigel said incontrovertibly.

'Perhaps.'

'Not very agreeable,' Sir Nigel said, 'but you know we couldn't let you go, could we, without taking a look?'

'Did you see anything?'

Sir Nigel gave the impression of abruptly moving downstream to a quieter reach and casting his line again.

'Don't let me stop you dressing, my dear fellow.' He looked vaguely around the room before choosing a strictly upright chair, then lowered himself on to it as though it were a tuffet which might 'give'. He began feeling in one of his large pockets – for a sandwich?

'Any news for me?'

'I expect Dr Cave will be along in a few minutes. He was caught by a rather garrulous patient.' He drew a large silver watch out of his pocket – for some reason it was tangled up in a piece of string. 'Have to meet my wife at Liverpool Street. Are *you* married?'

'No.'

'Oh well, one care the less. Children can be a great responsibility.'

'I have a child – but she lives a long way off.'

'A long way off? I see.'

'We haven't seen much of each other.'

'Doesn't care for England?'

'The colour-bar makes it difficult for her.' He realized how childish he sounded directly he had spoken, as though he had been trying to draw attention to himself by a bizarre confession, without even the satisfaction of success.

'Ah yes,' Sir Nigel said. 'Any brothers or sisters? You, I mean.'

'An elder brother. Why?'

'Oh well, I suppose it's all on the record,' Sir Nigel said, rolling in his line. He got up and made for the door. Wilditch sat on the bed with the tie over his knee. The door opened and Sir Nigel said, 'Ah, here's Dr Cave. Must run along now. I was just telling Mr Wilditch that I'll be seeing him again. You'll fix it, won't you?' and he was gone.

'Why should I see him again?' Wilditch asked and then, from Dr Cave's embarrassment, he saw the stupidity of the question. 'Oh yes, of course, you did find something?'

'It's really very lucky. If caught in time . . .'

'There's sometimes hope?'

'Oh, there's always hope.'

So, after all, Wilditch thought, I am – if I so choose – on the conveyor-belt again.

Dr Cave took an engagement-book out of his pocket and said briskly, 'Sir Nigel has given me a few dates. The tenth is difficult for the clinic, but the fifteenth – Sir Nigel doesn't think we should delay longer than the fifteenth.'

'Is he a great fisherman?'

'Fisherman? Sir Nigel? I have no idea.' Dr Cave looked

12

aggrieved, as though he were being shown an incorrect chart.
'Shall we say the fifteenth?'

'Perhaps I could tell you after the week-end. You see, I have
not made up my mind to stay as long as that in England.'

'I'm afraid I haven't properly conveyed to you that this
is serious, really serious. Your only chance – I repeat your
only chance,' he spoke like a telegram, 'is to have the obstruction removed in time.'

'And then, I suppose, life can go on for a few more years.'

'It's impossible to guarantee ... but there have been complete cures.'

'I don't want to appear dialectical,' Wilditch said, 'but I do
have to decide, don't I, whether I want my particular kind of
life prolonged.'

'It's the only one we have,' Dr Cave said.

'I see you are not a religious man – oh, please don't mis-
understand me, nor am I. I have no curiosity at all about the
future.'

3

The past was another matter. Wilditch remembered a leader
in the Civil War who rode from an undecided battle mortally
wounded. He revisited the house where he was born, the house
in which he was married, greeted a few retainers who did not
recognize his condition, seeing him only as a tired man upon a
horse, and finally – but Wilditch could not recollect how the
biography had ended: he saw only a figure of exhaustion
slumped over the saddle, as he also took, like Sir Nigel Sampson, a train from Liverpool Street. At Colchester he changed
onto the branch line to Winton, and suddenly summer began,
the kind of summer he always remembered as one of the con-
ditions of life at Winton. Days had become so much shorter
since then. They no longer began at six in the morning before
the world was awake.

Winton Hall had belonged, when Wilditch was a child, to
his uncle, who had never married, and every summer he lent
the house to Wilditch's mother. Winton Hall had been virtually
Wilditch's, until school cut the period short, from late June to
early September. In memory his mother and brother were

shadowy background figures. They were less established even than the machine upon the platform of 'the halt' from which he bought Fry's chocolates for a penny a bar: than the oak tree spreading over the green in front of the red-brick wall – under its shade as a child he had distributed apples to soldiers halted there in the hot August of 1914: the group of silver birches on the Winton lawn and the broken fountain, green with slime. In his memory he did not share the house with others: he owned it.

Nevertheless the house had been left to his brother not to him; he was far away when his uncle died and he had never returned since. His brother married, had children (for them the fountain had been mended), the paddock behind the vegetable garden and the orchard, where he used to ride the donkey, had been sold (so his brother had written to him) for building council-houses, but the hall and the garden which he had so scrupulously remembered nothing could change.

Why then go back now and see it in other hands? Was it that at the approach of death one must get rid of everything? If he had accumulated money he would now have been in the mood to distribute it. Perhaps the man who had ridden the horse around the countryside had not been saying goodbye, as his biographer imagined, to what he valued most: he had been ridding himself of illusions by seeing them again with clear and moribund eyes, so that he might be quite bankrupt when death came. He had the will to possess at that absolute moment nothing but his wound.

His brother, Wilditch knew, would be faintly surprised by this visit. He had become accustomed to the fact that Wilditch never came to Winton; they would meet at long intervals at his brother's club in London, for George was a widower by this time, living alone. He always talked to others of Wilditch as a man unhappy in the country, who needed a longer range and stranger people. It was lucky, he would indicate, that the house had been left to him, for Wilditch would probably have sold it in order to travel further. A restless man, never long in one place, no wife, no children, unless the rumours were true that in Africa ... or it might have been in the East ... Wilditch was well aware of how his brother spoke of him. His brother was the proud owner of the lawn, the goldfish-pond, the mended fountain, the laurel-path which they had known when they were children as the Dark Walk, the lake, the island ... Wilditch looked out at the flat hard East Anglian countryside, the meagre hedges and the stubbly grass, which had always seemed to him barren from the salt of Danish blood. All these years his brother had been in occupation, and yet he had no idea of what might lie underneath the garden.

4

The chocolate-machine had gone from Winton Halt, and the halt had been promoted – during the years of nationalization – to a station; the chimneys of a cement-factory smoked along the horizon and council-houses now stood three deep along the line.

Wilditch's brother waited in a Humber at the exit. Some familiar smell of coal-dust and varnish had gone from the waiting-room and it was a mere boy who took his ticket instead of a stooped and greying porter. In childhood nearly all the world is older than oneself.

'Hullo, George,' he said in remote greeting to the stranger at the wheel.

'How are things, William?' George asked as they ground on their way – it was part of his character as a countryman that he had never learnt how to drive a car well.

The long chalky slope of a small hill – the highest point before the Ural mountains he had once been told – led down to the village between the bristly hedges. On the left was an abandoned chalk-pit – it had been just as abandoned forty years ago, when he had climbed all over it looking for treasure, in the form of brown nuggets of iron pyrites which when broken showed an interior of starred silver.

'Do you remember hunting for treasure?'

'Treasure?' George said. 'Oh, you mean that iron stuff.'

Was it the long summer afternoons in the chalk-pit which had made him dream – or so vividly imagine – the discovery of a real treasure? If it was a dream it was the only dream he remembered from those years, or, if it was a story which he

had elaborated at night in bed, it must have been the final
effort of a poetic imagination that afterwards had been rigidly
controlled. In the various services which had over the years
taken him from one part of the world to another, imagination
was usually a quality to be suppressed. One's job was to provide facts, to a company (import and export), a newspaper, a
government department. Speculation was discouraged. Now
the dreaming child was dying of the same disease as the man.
He was so different from the child that it was odd to think the
child would not outlive him and go on to quite a different
destiny.

George said, 'You'll notice some changes, William. When
I had the new bathroom added, I found I had to disconnect
the pipes from the fountain. Something to do with pressure.
After all there are no children now to enjoy it.'

'It never played in my time either.'

'I had the tennis-lawn dug up during the war, and it hardly
seemed worth while to put it back.'

'I'd forgotten that there *was* a tennis-lawn.'

'Don't you remember it, between the pond and the gold-
fish-tank?'

'The pond? Oh, you mean the lake and the island.'

'Not much of a lake. You could jump on to the island with
a short run.'

'I had thought of it as much bigger.'

But all measurements had changed. Only for a dwarf does
the world remain the same size. Even the red-brick wall which
separated the garden from the village was lower than he remembered – a mere five feet, but in order to look over it in
those days he had always to scramble to the top of some old
stumps covered deep with ivy and dusty spiders' webs. There
was no sign of these when they drove in: everything was very
tidy everywhere, and a handsome piece of ironmongery had
taken the place of the swing-gate which they had ruined as
children.

'You keep the place up very well,' he said.

'I couldn't manage it without the market-garden. That en-
ables me to put the gardener's wages down as a professional
expense. I have a very good accountant.'

He was put into his mother's room with a view of the lawn and the silver birches; George slept in what had been his uncle's. The little bedroom next door which had once been his was now converted into a tiled bathroom – only the prospect was unchanged. He could see the laurel bushes where the Dark Walk began, but they were smaller too. Had the dying horseman found as many changes?

Sitting that night over coffee and brandy, during the long family pauses, Wilditch wondered whether as a child he could possibly have been so secretive as never to have spoken of his dream, his game, whatever it was. In his memory the adventure had lasted for several days. At the end of it he had found his way home in the early morning when everyone was asleep: there had been a dog called Joe who bounded towards him and sent him sprawling in the heavy dew of the lawn. Surely there must have been some basis of fact on which the legend had been built. Perhaps he had run away, perhaps he had been out all night – on the island in the lake or hidden in the Dark Walk – and during those hours he had invented the whole story.

Wilditch took a second glass of brandy and asked tentatively, 'Do you remember much of those summers when we were children here?' He was aware of something unconvincing in the question: the apparently harmless opening gambit of a wartime interrogation.

'I never cared for the place much in those days,' George said surprisingly. 'You were a secretive little bastard.'

'Secretive?'

'And uncooperative. I had a great sense of duty towards you, but you never realized that. In a year or two you were going to follow me to school. I tried to teach you the rudiments of cricket. You weren't interested. God knows what you were interested in.'

'Exploring?' Wilditch suggested, he thought with cunning.

'There wasn't much to explore in fourteen acres. You know, I had such plans for this place when it became mine. A swimming-pool where the tennis-lawn was – it's mainly potatoes now. I meant to drain the pond too – it breeds mosquitoes. Well, I've added two bathrooms and modernized the kitchen, and even that has cost me four acres of pasture. At the back of the house now you can hear the children caterwauling from the council-houses. It's all been a bit of a disappointment.'

'At least I'm glad you haven't drained the lake.'

'My dear chap, why go on calling it the lake? Have a look at it in the morning and you'll see the absurdity. The water's nowhere more than two feet deep.' He added, 'Oh well, the place won't outlive me. My children aren't interested, and the factories are beginning to come out this way. They'll get a reasonably good price for the land – I haven't much else to leave them.' He put some more sugar in his coffee. 'Unless, of course, you'd like to take it on when I am gone?'

'I haven't the money and anyway there's no cause to believe that I won't be dead first.'

'Mother was against my accepting the inheritance,' George said. 'She never liked the place.'

'I thought she loved her summers here.' The great gap between their memories astonished him. They seemed to be talking about different places and different people.

'It was terribly inconvenient, and she was always in trouble with the gardener. You remember Ernest? She said she had to wring every vegetable out of him. (By the way he's still alive, though retired of course – you ought to look him up in the morning. It would please him. He still feels he owns the place.) And then, you know, she always thought it would have been better for us if we could have gone to the seaside. She had an idea that she was robbing us of a heritage – buckets and spades and seawater-bathing. Poor mother, she couldn't afford to turn down Uncle Henry's hospitality. I think in her heart she blamed father for dying when he did without providing for holidays at the sea.'

'Did you talk it over with her in those days?'

'Oh no, not then. Naturally she had to keep a front before the children. But when I inherited the place – you were in Africa – she warned Mary and me about the difficulties. She had very decided views, you know, about any mysteries, and that turned her against the garden. Too much shrubbery, she said. She wanted everything to be very clear. Early Fabian training, I daresay.'

18

'It's odd. I don't seem to have known her very well.'

'You had a passion for hide-and-seek. She never liked that. Mystery again. She thought it a bit morbid. There was a time when we couldn't find you. You were away for hours.'

'Are you sure it was hours? Not a whole night?'

'I don't remember it at all myself. Mother told me.' They drank their brandy for a while in silence. Then George said, 'She asked Uncle Henry to have the Dark Walk cleared away. She thought it was unhealthy with all the spiders' webs, but he never did anything about it.'

'I'm surprised *you* didn't.'

'Oh, it was on my list, but other things had priority, and now it doesn't seem worth while to make more changes.' He yawned and stretched. 'I'm used to early bed. I hope you don't mind. Breakfast at 8.30?'

'Don't make any changes for me.'

'There's just one thing I forgot to show you. The flush is tricky in your bathroom.'

George led the way upstairs. He said, 'The local plumber didn't do a very good job. Now, when you've pulled this knob, you'll find the flush never quite finishes. You have to do it a second time – sharply like this.'

Wilditch stood at the window looking out. Beyond the Dark Walk and the space where the lake must be, he could see the splinters of light given off by the council-houses; through one gap in the laurels there was even a street-light visible, and he could hear the faint sound of television-sets joining together different programmes like the discordant murmur of a mob.

He said, 'That view would have pleased mother. A lot of the mystery gone.'

'I rather like it this way myself,' George said, 'on a winter's evening. It's a kind of companionship. As one gets older one doesn't want to feel quite alone on a sinking ship. Not being a churchgoer myself . . .' he added, leaving the sentence lying like a torso on its side.

'At least we haven't shocked mother in that way, either of us.'

'Sometimes I wish I'd pleased her, though, about the Dark Walk. And the pond – how she hated that pond too.'

'Why?'

'Perhaps because you liked to hide on the island. Secrecy and mystery again. Wasn't there something you wrote about it once? A story?'

'Me? A story? Surely not.'

'I don't remember the circumstances. I thought – in a school magazine? Yes, I'm sure of it now. She was very angry indeed and she wrote rude remarks in the margin with a blue pencil. I saw them somewhere once. Poor mother.'

George led the way into the bedroom. He said, 'I'm sorry there's no bedside light. It was smashed last week, and I haven't been into town since.'

'It's all right. I don't read in bed.'

'I've got some good detective-stories downstairs if you wanted one.'

'Mysteries?'

'Oh, mother never minded those. They came under the heading of puzzles. Because there was always an answer.'

Beside the bed was a small bookcase. He said, 'I brought some of mother's books here when she died and put them in her room. Just the ones that she had liked and no bookseller would take.' Wilditch made out a title, *My Apprenticeship* by Beatrice Webb. 'Sentimental, I suppose, but I didn't want actually to *throw away* her favourite books. Good night.' He repeated, 'I'm sorry about the light.'

'It really doesn't matter.'

George lingered at the door. He said, 'I'm glad to see you here, William. There were times when I thought you were avoiding the place.'

'Why should I?'

'Well, you know how it is. I never go to Harrods now because I was there with Mary a few days before she died.'

'Nobody has died here. Except Uncle Henry, I suppose.'

'No, of course not. But why did you, suddenly, decide to come?'

'A whim,' Wilditch said.

'I suppose you'll be going abroad again soon?'

'I suppose so.'

'Well, good night.' He closed the door.

Wilditch undressed, and then, because he felt sleep too far away, he sat down on the bed under the poor centre-light and looked along the rows of shabby books. He opened Mrs Beatrice Webb at some account of a trade union congress and put it back. (The foundations of the future Welfare State were being truly and uninterestingly laid.) There were a number of Fabian pamphlets heavily scored with the blue pencil which George had remembered. In one place Mrs Wilditch had detected an error of one decimal point in some statistics dealing with agricultural imports. What passionate concentration must have gone to that discovery. Perhaps because his own life was coming to an end, he thought how little of this, in the almost impossible event of a future, she would have carried with her. A fairy-story in such an event would be a more valuable asset than a Fabian graph, but his mother had not approved of fairy-stories. The only children's book on these shelves was a history of England. Against an enthusiastic account of the battle of Agincourt she had pencilled furiously,

> And what good came of it at last?
> Said little Peterkin.

The fact that his mother had quoted a poem was in itself remarkable.

The storm which he had left behind in London had travelled east in his wake and now overtook him in short gusts of wind and wet that slapped at the pane. He thought, for no reason, It will be a rough night on the island. He had been disappointed to discover from George that the origin of the dream which had travelled with him round the world was probably no more than a story invented for a school-magazine and forgotten again, and just as that thought occurred to him, he saw a bound volume called *The Warburian* on the shelf.

He took it out, wondering why his mother had preserved it, and found a page turned down. It was the account of a cricket-match against Lancing and Mrs Wilditch had scored the margin: 'Wilditch One did good work in deep field.' Another turned-down leaf produced a passage under the heading Debating Society: 'Wilditch One spoke succinctly to the

21

motion.' The motion was 'That this House has no belief in the social policies of His Majesty's Government'. So George in those days had been a Fabian too.

He opened the book at random this time and a letter fell out. It had a printed heading, Dean's House, Warbury, and it read, 'Dear Mrs Wilditch, I was sorry to receive your letter of the 3rd and to learn that you were displeased with the little fantasy published by your younger son in *The Warburian*. I think you take a rather extreme view of the tale which strikes me as quite a good imaginative exercise for a boy of thirteen. Obviously he has been influenced by the term's reading of *The Golden Age* – which after all, fanciful though it may be, was written by a governor of the Bank of England.' (Mrs Wilditch had made several blue exclamation marks in the margin – perhaps representing her view of the Bank.) 'Last term's *Treasure Island* too may have contributed. It is always our intention at Warbury to foster the imagination – which I think you rather harshly denigrate when you write of "silly fancies". We have scrupulously kept our side of the bargain, knowing how strongly you feel, and the boy is not "subjected", as you put it, to any religious instruction at all. Quite frankly, Mrs Wilditch, I cannot see any trace of religious feeling in this little fancy – I have read it through a second time before writing to you – indeed the treasure, I'm afraid, is only too material, and quite at the mercy of those "who break in and steal".'

Wilditch tried to find the place from which the letter had fallen, working back from the date of the letter. Eventually he found it: 'The Treasure on the Island' by W.W.

Wilditch began to read.

5

'In the middle of the garden there was a great lake and in the middle of the lake an island with a wood. Not everybody knew about the lake, for to reach it you had to find your way down a long dark walk, and not many people's nerves were strong enough to reach the end. Tom knew that he was likely to be undisturbed in that frightening region, and so it was there that he constructed a raft out of old packing cases, and one drear

*wet day when he knew that everybody would be shut in the
house, he dragged the raft to the lake and paddled it across
to the island. As far as he knew he was the first to land there
for centuries.*

'*It was all overgrown on the island, but from a map he had
found in an ancient sea-chest in the attic he made his measurements, three paces north from the tall umbrella pine in the
middle and then two paces to the right. There seemed to be
nothing but scrub, but he had brought with him a pick and a
spade and with the dint of almost superhuman exertions he un-
covered an iron ring sunk in the grass. At first he thought it
would be impossible to move, but by inserting the point of the
pick and levering it he raised a kind of stone lid and there
below, going into the darkness, was a long narrow passage.*

'*Tom had more than the usual share of courage, but even
he would not have ventured further if it had not been for the
parlous state of the family fortunes since his father had died.
His elder brother wanted to go to Oxford but for lack of
money he would probably have to sail before the mast, and the
house itself, of which his mother was passionately fond, was
mortgaged to the hilt to a man in the City called Sir Silas Ded-
ham whose name did not belie his nature.*'

Wilditch nearly gave up reading. He could not reconcile
this childish story with the dream which he remembered.
Only the 'drear wet night' seemed true as the bushes rustled
and dripped and the birches swayed outside. A writer, so he
had always understood, was supposed to order and enrich
the experience which was the source of his story, but in that
case it was plain that the young Wilditch's talents had not
been for literature. He read with growing irritation, wanting
to exclaim again and again to this thirteen-year-old ancestor
of his, 'But why did you leave that out? Why did you alter
this?'

'*The passage opened out into a great cave stacked from
floor to ceiling with gold bars and chests overflowing with
pieces of eight. There was a jewelled crucifix*' – Mrs Wilditch
had underlined the word in blue – '*set with precious stones
which had once graced the chapel of a Spanish galleon and
on a marble table were goblets of precious metal*'

23

But, as he remembered, it was an old kitchen-dresser, and there were no pieces of eight, no crucifix, and as for the Spanish galleon . . .

'*Tom thanked the kindly Providence which had led him first to the map in the attic*' (but there had been no map. Wilditch wanted to correct the story, page by page, much as his mother had done with her blue pencil '*and then to this rich treasure trove*' (his mother had written in the margin, referring to the kindly Providence, 'No trace of religious feeling! !'). '*He filled his pockets with the pieces of eight and taking one bar under each arm, he made his way back along the passage. He intended to keep his discovery secret and slowly day by day to transfer the treasures to the cupboard in his room, thus surprising his mother at the end of the holidays with all this sudden wealth. He got safely home unseen by anyone and that night in bed he counted over his new riches while outside it rained and rained. Never had he heard such a storm. It was as though the wicked spirit of his old pirate ancestor raged against him*' (Mrs Wilditch had written, 'Eternal punishment I suppose!') '*and indeed the next day, when he returned to the island in the lake, whole trees had been uprooted and now lay across the entrance to the passage. Worse still there had been a landslide, and now the cavern must lie hidden forever below the waters of the lake. However,*' the young Wilditch had added briefly forty years ago, '*the treasure already recovered was sufficient to save the family home and send his brother to Oxford.*'

Wilditch undressed and got into bed, then lay on his back listening to the storm. What a trivial conventional day-dream W.W. had constructed – out of what? There had been no attic-room – probably no raft: these were preliminaries which did not matter, but why had W.W. so falsified the adventure itself? Where was the man with the beard? The old squawking woman? Of course it had all been a dream, it could have been nothing else but a dream, but a dream too was an experience, the images of a dream had their own integrity, and he felt professional anger at this false report just as his mother had felt at the mistake in the Fabian statistics.

All the same, while he lay there in his mother's bed and

thought of her rigid interrogation of W.W.'s story, another
theory of the falsifications came to him, perhaps a juster
one. He remembered that agents parachuted into France during the bad years after 1940 had been made to memorize a
cover-story which they could give, in case of torture, with
enough truth in it to be checked. Perhaps forty years ago the
pressure to tell had been almost as great on W.W., so that
he had been forced to find relief in fantasy. Well, an agent
dropped into occupied territory was always given a time-
limit after capture. 'Keep the interrogators at bay with silence
or lies for just so long, and then you may tell all.' The time-
limit had surely been passed in his case a long time ago, his
mother was beyond the possibility of hurt, and Wilditch for
the first time deliberately indulged his passion to remember.

He got out of bed and, after finding some notepaper
stamped, presumably for income-tax purposes, Winton Small
Holdings Limited, in the drawer of the desk, he began to write
an account of what he had found – or dreamed that he found
– under the garden of Winton Hall. The summer night was
nosing wetly around the window just as it had done fifty years
ago, but, as he wrote, it began to turn grey and recede; the
trees of the garden became visible, so that, when he looked
up after some hours from his writing, he could see the shape
of the broken fountain and what he supposed were the laurels
in the Dark Walk, looking like old men humped against the
weather.

PART TWO

1

Never mind how I came to the island in the lake, never mind
whether in fact, as my brother says, it is a shallow pond with
water only two feet deep (I suppose a raft can be launched
on two feet of water, and certainly I must have always come
to the lake by way of the Dark Walk, so that it is not at all
unlikely that I built my raft there). Never mind what hour
it was – I think it was evening, and I had hidden, as I remember it, in the Dark Walk because George had not got the

courage to search for me there. The evening turned to rain, just as it's raining now, and George must have been summoned into the house for shelter. He would have told my mother that he couldn't find me and she must have called from the upstair windows, front and back – perhaps it was the occasion George spoke about tonight. I am not sure of these facts, they are plausible only, I can't yet *see* what I'm describing. But I know that I was not to find George and my mother again for many days . . . It cannot, whatever George says, have been less than three days and nights that I spent below the ground. Could he really have forgotten so inexplicable an experience?

And here I am already checking my story as though it were something which had really happened, for what possible relevance has George's memory to the events of a dream?

I dreamed that I crossed the lake, I dreamed . . . that is the only certain fact and I must cling to it, the fact that I dreamed. How my poor mother would grieve if she could know that, even for a moment, I had begun to think of these events as true . . . but, of course, if it were possible for her to know what I am thinking now, there would be no limit to the area of possibility. I dreamed then that I crossed the water (either by swimming – I could already swim at seven years old – or by wading if the lake is really as small as George makes out, or by paddling a raft) and scrambled up the slope of the island. I can remember grass, scrub, brushwood, and at last a wood. I would describe it as a forest if I had not already seen, in the height of the garden-wall, how age diminishes size. I don't remember the umbrella-pine which W.W. described – I suspect he stole the sentinel-tree from *Treasure Island*, but I do know that when I got into the wood I was completely hidden from the house and the trees were close enough together to protect me from the rain. Quite soon I was lost, and yet how could I have been lost if the lake were no bigger than a pond, and the island therefore not much larger than the top of a kitchen-table?

Again I find myself checking my memories as though they were facts. A dream does not take account of size. A puddle can contain a continent, and a clump of trees stretch in sleep

to the world's edge. I dreamed, I *dreamed* that I was lost and
that night began to fall. I was not frightened. It was as though
even at seven I was accustomed to travel. All the rough jour-
neys of the future were already in me then, like a muscle
which had only to develop. I curled up among the roots of the
trees and slept. When I woke I could still hear the pit-pat of
the rain in the upper branches and the steady zing of an insect
near by. All these noises come as clearly back to me now as the
sound of the rain on the parked cars outside the clinic in
Wimpole Street, the music of yesterday.

The moon had risen and I could see more easily around me.
I was determined to explore further before the morning came,
for then an expedition would certainly be sent in search of
me. I knew, from the many books of exploration George had
read to me, of the danger to a person lost of walking in circles
until eventually he dies of thirst or hunger, so I cut a cross
in the bark of the tree (I had brought a knife with me that
contained several blades, a small saw and an instrument for
removing pebbles from horses' hooves). For the sake of future
reference I named the place where I had slept Camp Hope.
I had no fear of hunger, for I had apples in both pockets, and
as for thirst I had only to continue in a straight line and I
would come eventually to the lake again where the water was
sweet, or at worst a little brackish. I go into all these details,
which W.W. unaccountably omitted, to test my memory. I
had forgotten until now how far or how deeply it extended.
Had W.W. forgotten or was he afraid to remember?

I had gone a little more than three hundred yards – I paced
the distances and marked every hundred paces or so on a
tree – it was the best I could do, without proper surveying
instruments, for the map I already planned to draw – when I
reached a great oak of apparently enormous age with roots
that coiled away above the surface of the ground. (I was
reminded of those roots once in Africa where they formed a
kind of shrine for a fetish – a seated human figure made out
of a gourd and palm fronds and unidentifiable vegetable matter gone rotten in the rains and a great penis of bamboo.
Coming on it suddenly, I was frightened, or was it the memory
that it brought back which scared me?) Under one of these

27

roots the earth had been disturbed; somebody had shaken a mound of charred tobacco from a pipe and a sequin glistened like a snail in the moist moonlight. I struck a match to examine the ground closer and saw the imprint of a foot in a patch of loose earth – it was pointing at the tree from a few inches away and it was as solitary as the print Crusoe found on the sands of another island. It was as though a one-legged man had taken a leap out of the bushes straight at the tree.

Pirate ancestor! What nonsense W.W. had written, or had he converted the memory of that stark frightening footprint into some comforting thought of the kindly scoundrel, Long John Silver, and his wooden leg?

I stood astride the imprint and stared up the tree, half expecting to see a one-legged man perched like a vulture among the branches. I listened and there was no sound except last night's rain dripping from leaf to leaf. Then – I don't know why – I went down on my knees and peered among the roots. There was no iron ring, but one of the roots formed an arch more than two feet high like the entrance to a cave. I put my head inside and lit another match – I couldn't see the back of the cave.

It's difficult to remember that I was only seven years old. To the self we remain always the same age. I was afraid at first to venture further, but so would any grown man have been, any one of the explorers I thought of as my peers. My brother had been reading aloud to me a month before from a book called *The Romance of Australian Exploration* – my own powers of reading had not advanced quite as far as that, but my memory was green and retentive and I carried in my head all kinds of new images and evocative words – aboriginal, sextant, Murumbidgee, Stony Desert, and the points of the compass with their big capital letters E.S.E. and N.N.W. had an excitement they have never quite lost. They were like the figure on a watch which at last comes round to pointing the important hour. I was comforted by the thought that Sturt had been sometimes daunted and that Burke's bluster often hid his fear. Now, kneeling by the cave, I remembered a cavern which George Grey, another hero of mine, had entered and how suddenly he had come on the figure of a man ten feet high painted on the wall, clothed from the chin down to the ankles in a red garment. I don't know why, but I was more afraid of that painting than I was of the aborigines who killed Burke, and the fact that the feet and hands which protruded from the garment were said to be badly executed added to the terror. A foot which looked like a foot was only human, but my imagination could play endlessly with the faults of the painter – a club-foot, a claw-foot, the worm-like toes of a bird. Now I associated this strange footprint with the ill-executed painting, and I hesitated a long time before I got the courage to crawl into the cave under the root. Before doing so, in reference to the footprint, I gave the spot the name of Friday's Cave.

2

For some yards I could not even get upon my knees, the roof grated my hair, and it was impossible for me in that position to strike another match. I could only inch along like a worm, making an ideograph in the dust. I didn't notice for a while in the darkness that I was crawling down a long slope, but I could feel on either side of me roots rubbing my shoulders like the banisters of a staircase. I was creeping through the branches of an underground tree in a mole's world. Then the impediments were passed – I was out the other side; I banged my head again on the earth-wall and found that I could rise to my knees. But I nearly toppled down again, for I had not realized how steeply the ground sloped. I was more than a man's height below ground and, when I struck a match, I could see no finish to the long gradient going down. I cannot help feeling a little proud that I continued on my way, on my knees this time, though I suppose it is arguable whether one can really show courage in a dream.

I was halted again by a turn in the path, and this time I found I could rise to my feet after I had struck another match. The track had flattened out and ran horizontally. The air was stuffy with an odd disagreeable smell like cabbage cooking, and I wanted to go back. I remembered how miners carried canaries with them in cages to test the freshness of the air, and I wished I had thought of bringing our own canary with me which had accompanied us to Winton Hall – it would have been company too in that dark tunnel with its tiny song. There was something, I remembered, called coal-damp which caused explosions, and this passage was certainly damp enough. I must be nearly under the lake by this time, and I thought to myself that, if there was an explosion, the waters of the lake would pour in and drown me.

I blew out my match at the idea, but all the same I continued on my way in the hope that I might come on an exit a little easier than the long crawl back through the roots of the trees.

Suddenly ahead of me something whistled, only it was less like a whistle than a hiss: it was like the noise a kettle makes when it is on the boil. I thought of snakes and wondered whether some giant serpent had made its nest in the tunnel. There was something fatal to man called a Black Mamba ... I stood stock-still and held my breath, while the whistling went on and on for a long while, before it whined out into nothing. I would have given anything then to have been safe back in bed in the room next to my mother's, with the electric-light switch close to my hand and the firm bed-end at my feet. There was a strange clanking sound and a duck-like quack. I couldn't bear the darkness any more and I lit another match, reckless of coal-damp. It shone on a pile of old news-papers and nothing else – it was strange to find I had not been the first person here. I called out 'Hullo!' and my voice went on in diminishing echoes down the long passage. Nobody answered, and when I picked up one of the papers I saw it was no proof of a human presence. It was the *East Anglian Observer* for April 5th 1885 – 'with which is incorporated the *Colchester Guardian*'. It's funny how even the date remains in my mind and the Victorian Gothic type of the titling. There was a faint fishy smell about it as though – oh, eons ago – it had been wrapped around a bit of prehistoric cod. The match burnt my fingers and went out. Perhaps I was the first to come here for all those years, but suppose whoever had brought those papers were lying somewhere dead in the tunnel ...

Then I had an idea. I made a torch of the paper in my hand, tucked the others under my arm to serve me later, and with the stronger light advanced more boldly down the passage. After all wild beasts – so George had read to me – and serpents too in all likelihood – were afraid of fire, and my fear of an explosion had been driven out by the greater terror of what I might find in the dark. But it was not a snake or a leopard or a tiger or any other cavern-haunting animal that I saw when I turned the second corner. Scrawled with the simplicity of ancient man upon the left-hand wall of the passage – done with a sharp tool like a chisel – was the outline of a gigantic fish. I held up my paper-torch higher and saw the remains of lettering either half-obliterated or in a language I didn't know.

$$\int \cdot c_\Lambda \quad \lrcorner^\frown \quad c_{\vdash_\Lambda} \, \frown$$

I was trying to make sense of the symbols when a hoarse voice out of sight called, 'Maria, Maria'.

I stood very still and the newspaper burned down in my hand. 'Is that you, Maria?' the voice said. It sounded to me very angry. 'What kind of a trick are you playing? What's the clock say? Surely it's time for my broth.' And then I heard again that strange quacking sound which I had heard before. There was a long whispering and after that silence.

3

I suppose I was relieved that there were human beings and not wild beasts down the passage, but what kind of human beings could they be except criminals hiding from justice or gypsies who are notorious for stealing children? I was afraid to think what they might do to anyone who discovered their secret. It was also possible, of course, that I had come on the home of some aboriginal tribe ... I stood there unable to make up my mind whether to go on or turn back. It was not a problem which my Australian peers could help me to solve, for they had sometimes found the aboriginals friendly folk who gave them fish (I thought of the fish on the wall) and

sometimes enemies who attacked with spears. In any case –
whether these were criminals or gypsies or aboriginals – I had
only a pocket-knife for my defence. I think it showed the
true spirit of an explorer that in spite of my fears I thought
of the map I must one day draw if I survived and so named
this spot Camp Indecision.

My indecision was solved for me. An old woman appeared
suddenly and noiselessly around the corner of the passage.
She wore an old blue dress which came down to her ankles
covered with sequins, and her hair was grey and straggly and
she was going bald on top. She was every bit as surprised as
I was. She stood there gaping at me and then she opened her
mouth and squawked. I learned later that she had no roof to
her mouth and was probably saying, 'Who are you?' but then
I thought it was some foreign tongue she spoke – perhaps
aboriginee – and I replied with an attempt at assurance, 'I'm
English.'

The hoarse voice out of sight said, 'Bring him along here,
Maria.'

The old woman took a step towards me, but I couldn't
bear the thought of being touched by her hands, which
were old and curved like a bird's and covered with the brown
patches that Ernest, the gardener, had told me were 'grave-
marks'; her nails were very long and filled with dirt. Her
dress was dirty too and I thought of the sequin I'd seen
outside and imagined her scrabbling home through the roots
of the tree. I backed up against the side of the passage
and somehow squeezed around her. She quacked after me,
but I went on. Round a second – or perhaps a third –
corner I found myself in a great cave some eight feet high.
On what I thought was a throne, but I later realized was an old
lavatory-seat, sat a big old man with a white beard yellowing
round the mouth from what I suppose now to have been
nicotine. He had one good leg, but the right trouser was
sewn up and looked stuffed like a bolster. I could see him
quite well because an oil-lamp stood on a kitchen-table, beside
a carving-knife and two cabbages, and his face came vividly
back to me the other day when I was reading Darwin's
description of a carrier-pigeon: 'Greatly elongated eyelids, very

large external orifices to the nostrils, and a wide gape of mouth.'

He said, 'And who would you be and what are you doing here and why are you burning my newspaper?'

The old woman came squawking around the corner and then stood still behind me, barring my retreat.

I said, 'My name's William Wilditch, and I come from Winton Hall.'

'And where's Winton Hall?' he asked, never stirring from his lavatory-seat.

'Up there,' I said and pointed at the roof of the cave.

'That means precious little,' he said. 'Why, everything is up there, China and all America too and the Sandwich Islands.'

'I suppose so,' I said. There was a kind of reason in most of what he said, as I came to realize later.

'But down here there's only us. We are exclusive,' he said, 'Maria and me.'

I was less frightened of him now. He spoke English. He was a fellow-countryman. I said, 'If you'll tell me the way out I'll be going on my way.'

'What's that you've got under your arm?' he asked me sharply. 'More newspapers?'

'I found them in the passage . . .'

'Finding's not keeping here,' he said, 'whatever it may be up there in China. You'll soon discover that. Why, that's the last lot of papers Maria brought in. What would we have for reading if we let you go and pinch them?'

'I didn't mean . . .'

'Can you read?' he asked, not listening to my excuses.

'If the words aren't too long.'

'Maria can read, but she can't see very well any more than I can, and she can't articulate much.'

Maria went kwahk, kwahk behind me, like a bull-frog it seems to me now, and I jumped. If that was how she read I wondered how he could understand a single word. He said, 'Try a piece.'

'What do you mean?'

'Can't you understand plain English? You'll have to work for your supper down here.'

'But it's not supper-time. It's still early in the morning,' I said.

'What o'clock is it, Maria?'

'Kwahk,' she said.

'Six. That's supper-time.'

'But it's six in the morning, not the evening.'

'How do you know? Where's the light? There aren't such things as mornings and evenings here.'

'Then how do you ever wake up?' I asked. His beard shook as he laughed. 'What a shrewd little shaver he is,' he exclaimed. 'Did you hear that, Maria? "How do you ever wake up?" he said. All the same you'll find that life here isn't all beer and skittles and who's your Uncle Joe. If you are clever, you'll learn and if you are not clever . . .' He brooded morosely. 'We are deeper here than any grave was ever dug to bury secrets in. Under the earth or over the earth, it's there you'll find all that matters.' He added angrily, 'Why aren't you reading a piece as I told you to? If you are to stay with us, you've got to jump to it.'

'I don't want to stay.'

'You think you can just take a peek, is that it? and go away. You are wrong – but take all the peek you want and then get on with it.'

I didn't like the way he spoke, but all the same I did as he suggested. There was an old chocolate-stained chest of drawers, a tall kitchen-cupboard, a screen covered with scraps and transfers, and a wooden crate which perhaps served Maria for a chair, and another larger one for a table. There was a cooking-stove with a kettle pushed to one side, steaming yet. That would have caused the whistle I had heard in the passage. I could see no sign of any bed, unless a heap of potato-sacks against the wall served that purpose. There were a lot of bread-crumbs on the earth-floor and a few bones had been swept into a corner as though awaiting interment.

'And now,' he said, 'show your young paces. I've yet to see whether you are worth your keep.'

'But I don't want to be kept,' I said. 'I really don't. It's time I went home.'

'Home's where a man lies down,' he said, 'and this is where

34

you'll lie from now on. Now take the first page that comes and read to me. I want to hear the news.'

'But the paper's nearly fifty years old,' I said. 'There's no news in it.'

'News is news however old it is.' I began to notice a way he had of talking in general statements like a lecturer or a prophet. He seemed to be less interested in conversation than in the recital of some articles of belief, odd crazy ones, perhaps, yet somehow I could never put my finger convincingly on an error. 'A cat's a cat even when it's a dead cat. We get rid of it when it's smelly, but news never smells, however long it's dead. News keeps. And it comes round again when you least expect. Like thunder.'

I opened the paper at random and read: 'Garden fête at the Grange. The fête at the Grange, Long Wilson, in aid of Distressed Gentlewomen was opened by Lady (Isobel) Montgomery.' I was a bit put out by the long words coming so quickly, but I acquitted myself with fair credit. He sat on the lavatory-seat with his head sunk a little, listening with attention. 'The Vicar presided at the White Elephant Stall.'

The old man said with satisfaction, 'They are royal beasts.'

'But these were not really elephants,' I said.

'A stall is part of a stable, isn't it? What do you want a stable for if they aren't real? Go on. Was it a good fate or an evil fate?'

'It's not that kind of fate either,' I said.

'There's no other kind,' he said. 'It's your fate to read to me. It's *her* fate to talk like a frog, and mine to listen because my eyesight's bad. This is an underground fate we suffer from here, and that was a garden fate – but it all comes to the same fate in the end.' It was useless to argue with him and I read on: 'Unfortunately the festivities were brought to an untimely close by a heavy rainstorm.'

Maria gave a kwahk that sounded like a malicious laugh, and 'You see,' the old man said, as though what I had read proved somehow he was right, 'that's fate for you.'

'The evening's events had to be transferred indoors, including the Morris dancing and the Treasure Hunt.'

'Treasure Hunt?' the old man asked sharply.

'That's what it says here.'

'The impudence of it,' he said. 'The sheer impudence. Maria, did you hear that?'

She kwahked – this time, I thought, angrily.

'It's time for my broth,' he said with deep gloom, as though he were saying, 'It's time for my death.'

'It happened a long time ago,' I said, trying to soothe him.

'Time,' he exclaimed, 'you can — time,' using a word quite unfamiliar to me which I guessed – I don't know how – was one that I could not with safety use myself when I returned home. Maria had gone behind the screen – there must have been other cupboards there, for I heard her opening and shutting doors and clanking pots and pans.

I whispered to him quickly, 'Is she your luba?'

'Sister, wife, mother, daughter,' he said, 'what difference does it make? Take your choice. She's a woman, isn't she?' He brooded there on the lavatory-seat like a king on a throne. 'There are two sexes,' he said. 'Don't try to make more than two with definitions.' The statement sank into my mind with the same heavy mathematical certainty with which later on at school I learned the rule of Euclid about the sides of an isosceles triangle. There was a long silence.

'I think I'd better be going,' I said, shifting up and down. Maria came in. She carried a dish marked Fido filled with hot broth. Her husband, her brother, whatever he was, nursed it on his lap a long while before he drank it. He seemed to be lost in thought again, and I hesitated to disturb him. All the same, after a while, I tried again.

'They'll be expecting me at home.'

'Home?'

'Yes.'

'You couldn't have a better home than this,' he said. 'You'll see. In a bit of time – a year or two – you'll settle down well enough.'

I tried my best to be polite. 'It's very nice here, I'm sure, but . . .'

'It's no use your being restless. I didn't ask you to come, did I, but now you are here, you'll stay. Maria's a great hand with cabbage. You won't suffer any hardship.'

'But I can't stay. My mother . . .'

'Forget your mother and your father too. If you need any-thing from up there Maria will fetch it down for you.'

'But I can't stay here.'

'Can't's not a word that you can use to the likes of me.'

'But you haven't any right to keep me . . .'

'And what right had you to come busting in like a thief, getting Maria all disturbed when she was boiling my broth?'

'I couldn't stay here with you. It's not – sanitary.' I don't know how I managed to get that word out. 'I'd die . . .'

'There's no need to talk of dying down here. No one's ever died here, and you've no reason to believe that anyone ever will. We aren't dead, are we, and we've lived a long long time, Maria and me. You don't know how lucky you are. There's treasure here beyond all the riches of Asia. One day, if you don't go disturbing Maria, I'll show you. You know what a millionaire is?' I nodded. 'They aren't one quarter as rich as Maria and me. And they die too, and where's their treasure then? Rockefeller's gone and Fred's gone and Columbus. I sit here and just read about dying – it's an entertainment that's all. You'll find in all those papers what they call an obituary – there's one about a Lady Caroline Winterbottom that made Maria laugh and me. It's summerbottoms we have here, I said, all the year round, sitting by the stove.'

Maria kwahked in the background, and I began to cry more as a way of interrupting him than because I was really frightened.

It's extraordinary how vividly after all these years I can remember that man and the words he spoke. If they were to dig down now on the island below the roots of the tree, I would half expect to find him sitting there still on the old lavatory-seat which seemed to be detached from any pipes or drainage and serve no useful purpose, and yet, if he had really existed, he must have passed his century a long time ago. There was something of a monarch about him and something, as I said, of a prophet and something of the gardener my mother disliked and of a policeman in the next village; his expres-sions were often countrylike and coarse, but his ideas seemed to move on a deeper level, like roots spreading below a layer of compost. I could sit here now in this room for hours remembering the things he said – I haven't made out the sense of them all yet: they are stored in my memory like a code uncracked which waits for a clue or an inspiration.

He said to me sharply, 'We don't need salt here. There's too much as it is. You taste any bit of earth and you'll find it salt. We live in salt. We are pickled, you might say, in it. Look at Maria's hands, and you'll see the salt in the cracks.'

I stopped crying at once and looked (my attention could always be caught by bits of irrelevant information), and, true enough, there seemed to be grey-white seams running between her knuckles.

'You'll turn salty too in time,' he said encouragingly and drank his broth with a good deal of noise.

I said, 'But I really am going, Mr . . .'

'You can call me Javitt,' he said, 'but only because it's not my real name. You don't believe I'd give you that, do you? And Maria's not Maria – it's just a sound she answers to, you understand me, like Jupiter.'

'No.'

'If you had a dog called Jupiter, you wouldn't believe he was really Jupiter, would you?'

'I've got a dog called Joe.'

'The same applies,' he said and drank his soup. Sometimes I think that in no conversation since have I found the interest I discovered in those inconsequent sentences of his to which I listened during the days (I don't know how many) that I spent below the garden. Because, of course, I didn't leave that day. Javitt had his way.

He might be said to have talked me into staying, though if I had proved obstinate I have no doubt at all that Maria would have blocked my retreat, and certainly I would not have fancied struggling to escape through the musty folds of her clothes. That was the strange balance – to and fro – of those days; half the time I was frightened as though I were caged in a nightmare and half the time I only wanted to laugh freely and happily at the strangeness of his speech and the novelty of his ideas. It was as if, for those hours or days, the only important things in life were two, laughter and fear. (Perhaps the same ambivalence was there when I first began to know a woman.) There are people whose laughter has always a sense of superiority, but it was Javitt who taught me that laughter is more often a sign of equality, of pleasure and not of malice. He sat there on his lavatory-seat and he said, 'I shit dead stuff every day, do I? How wrong you are.' (I was already laughing because that was a word I knew to be obscene and I had never heard it spoken before.) 'Everything that comes out of me is alive, I tell you. It's squirming around there, germs and bacilli and the like, and it goes into the ground like a womb, and it comes out somewhere, I daresay, like my daughter did – I forgot I haven't told you about her.'

'Is she here?' I said with a look at the curtain, wondering what monstrous woman would next emerge.

'Oh, no, she went upstairs a long time ago.'

'Perhaps I could take her a message from you,' I said cunningly.

He looked at me with contempt. 'What kind of a message,' he asked, 'could the likes of you take to the likes of her?' He must have seen the motive behind my offer, for he reverted to the fact of my imprisonment. 'I'm not unreasonable,' he said, 'I'm not one to make hailstorms in harvest time, but if you went back up there you'd talk about me and Maria and the treasure we've got, and people would come digging.'

'I swear I'd say nothing' (and at least I have kept that promise, whatever others I have broken, through all the years).

'You talk in your sleep maybe. A boy's never alone. You've got a brother, I daresay, and soon you'll be going to school and hinting at things to make you seem important. There are plenty of ways of keeping an oath and breaking it in the same moment. Do you know what I'd do then? If they came searching? I'd go further in.'

Maria kwahk-kwahked her agreement where she listened from somewhere behind the curtains.

'What do you mean?'

'Give me a hand to get off this seat,' he said. He pressed his hand down on my shoulder and it was like a mountain heaving. I looked at the lavatory seat and I could see that it had been placed exactly to cover a hole which went down down down out of sight. 'A moit of the treasure's down there already,' he said, 'but I wouldn't let the bastards enjoy what they could find here. There's a little matter of subsidence I've got fixed up so that they'd never see the light of day again.'

'But what would you do below there for food?'

'We've got tins enough for another century or two,' he said. 'You'd be surprised at what Maria's stored away there. We don't use tins up here because there's always broth and cabbage and that's more healthy and keeps the scurvy off, but we've no more teeth to lose and our gums are fallen as it is, so if we had to fall back on tins we would. Why, there's hams and chickens and red salmons' eggs and butter and steak-and-kidney pies and caviar, venison too and marrow-bones, I'm forgetting the fish – cods' roe and sole in white wine, langouste legs, sardines, bloaters, and herrings in tomato-sauce, and all the fruits that ever grew, apples, pears, strawberries, figs, raspberries, plums and greengages and passion fruit, mangoes, grapefruit, loganberries and cherries, mulberries too and sweet things from Japan, not to speak of vegetables, Indian corn and taties, salsify and spinach and that thing they call endive, asparagus, peas and the hearts of bamboo, and I've left out our old friend the tomato.' He lowered himself heavily back on to his seat above the great hole going down.

'You must have enough for two lifetimes,' I said.

'There's means of getting more,' he added darkly, so that I pictured other channels delved through the undersoil of the garden like the section of an ant's nest, and I remembered the sequin on the island and the single footprint.

Perhaps all this talk of food had reminded Maria of her duties because she came quacking out from behind her dusty curtain, carrying two bowls of broth, one medium size for me and one almost as small as an egg-cup for herself. I tried politely to take the small one, but she snatched it away from me.

'You don't have to bother about Maria,' the old man said. 'She's been eating food for more years than you've got weeks. She knows her appetite.'

'What do you cook with?' I asked.

'Calor,' he said.

That was an odd thing about this adventure or rather this dream: fantastic though it was, it kept coming back to ordinary life with simple facts like that. The man could never, if I really thought it out, have existed all those years below the earth, and yet the cooking, as I seem to remember it, was done on a cylinder of calor-gas.

The broth was quite tasty and I drank it to the end. When I had finished I fidgeted about on the wooden box they had given me for a seat – nature was demanding something for which I was too embarrassed to ask aid.

'What's the matter with you?' Javitt said. 'Chair not comfortable?'

'Oh, it's very comfortable,' I said.

'Perhaps you want to lie down and sleep?'

'No.'

'I'll show you something which will give you dreams,' he said. 'A picture of my daughter.'

'I want to do number one,' I blurted out.

'Oh, is that all?' Javitt said. He called to Maria, who was still clattering around behind the curtain, 'The boy wants to piss. Fetch him the golden po.' Perhaps my eyes showed interest, for he added to me diminishingly, with the wave of a hand, 'It's the least of my treasures.'

All the same it was remarkable enough in my eyes, and I can remember it still, a veritable chamber-pot of gold. Even the young dauphin of France on that long road back from Varennes with his father had only a silver cup at his service. I would have been more embarrassed, doing what I called number one in front of the old man Javitt, if I had not been so impressed by the pot. It lent the everyday affair the importance of a ceremony, almost of a sacrament. I can remember the tinkle in the pot like far-away chimes as though a gold surface resounded differently from china or base metal.

Javitt reached behind him to a shelf stacked with old papers and picked one out. He said, 'Now you look at that and tell me what you think.'

It was a kind of magazine I'd never seen before – full of pictures which are now called cheese-cake. I have no earlier memory of a woman's unclothed body, or as nearly unclothed as made no difference to me then, in the skintight black costume. One whole page was given up to a Miss Ramsgate, shot from all angles. She was the favourite contestant for something called Miss England and might later go on, if she were successful, to compete for the title of Miss Europe, Miss World and after that Miss Universe. I stared at her as though I wanted to memorize her for ever. And that is exactly what I did.

'That's our daughter,' Javitt said.

'And did she become . . .'

'She was launched,' he said with pride and mystery, as though he were speaking of some moon-rocket which had at last after many disappointments risen from the pad and soared to outer space. I looked at the photograph, at the wise eyes and the inexplicable body, and I thought, with all the ignorance children have of age and generations, I never want to marry anybody but her. Maria put her hand through the curtains and quacked, and I thought, she would be my mother then, but not a hoot did I care. With that girl for my wife I could take anything, even school and growing up and life. And perhaps I could have taken them, if I had ever succeeded in finding her.

Again my thoughts are interrupted. For if I am remembering a vivid dream – and dreams do stay in all their detail far longer than we realize – how would I have known at that age about such absurdities as beauty-contests? A dream can only contain what one has experienced, or, if you have sufficient faith in Jung, what our ancestors have experienced. But calorgas and the Ramsgate Beauty Queen? . . . They are not ancestral memories, nor the memories of a child of seven. Certainly my mother did not allow us to buy with our meagre pocket-money – sixpence a week? – such papers as that. And yet the image is there, caught once and for all, not only the expression of the eyes, but the expression of the body too, the particular tilt of the breasts, the shallow scoop of the navel like something carved in sand, the little trim buttocks – the dividing line swung between them close and regular like the single sweep of a pencil. Can a child of seven fall in love for

life with a body? And there is a further mystery which did not
occur to me then: how could a couple as old as Javitt and
Maria have had a daughter so young in the period when such
contests were the vogue?

'She's a beauty,' Javitt said, 'you'll never see her like where
your folks live. Things grow differently underground, like a
mole's coat. I ask you where there's softness softer than that?'
I'm not sure whether he was referring to the skin of his
daughter or the coat of the mole.

I sat on the golden po and looked at the photograph and
listened to Javitt as I would have listened to my own father
if I had possessed one. His sayings are fixed in my memory
like the photograph. Gross some of them seem now, but they
did not appear gross to me then when even the graffiti on walls
were innocent. Except when he called me 'boy' or 'snapper'
or something of the kind he seemed unaware of my age: it
was not that he talked to me as an equal but as someone from
miles away, looking down from his old lavatory-seat to my
golden po, from so far away that he couldn't distinguish my
age, or perhaps he was so old that anyone under a century
or so seemed much alike to him. All that I write here was not
said at that moment. There must have been many days or
nights of conversation – you couldn't down there tell the difference – and now I dredge the sentences up, in no particular
order, just as they come to mind, sitting at my mother's desk
so many years later.

4

'You laugh at Maria and me. You think we look ugly. I tell
you she could have been painted if she had chosen by some
of the greatest – there's one that painted women with three
eyes – she'd have suited him. But she knew how to tunnel in
the earth like me, when to appear and when not to appear. It's
a long time now that we've been alone down here. It gets more
dangerous all the time – if you can speak of time – on the
upper floor. But don't think it hasn't happened before. But
when I remember . . .' But what he remembered has gone from
my head, except only his concluding phrase and a sense of
desolation: 'Looking round at all those palaces and towers,

you'd have thought they'd been made like a child's castle of the desert-sand.'

'In the beginning you had a name only the man or woman knew who pulled you out of your mother. Then there was a name for the tribe to call you by. That was of little account, but of more account all the same than the name you had with strangers; and there was a name used in the family – by your pa and ma if it's those terms you call them by nowadays. The only name without any power at all was the name you used to strangers. That's why I call myself Javitt to you, but the name the man who pulled me out knew – that was so secret I had to keep him as a friend for life, so that he wouldn't even tell me because of the responsibility it would bring – I might let it slip before a stranger. Up where you come from they've begun to forget the power of the name. I wouldn't be surprised if you only had the one name and what's the good of a name everyone knows? Do you suppose even I feel secure here with my treasure and all – because, you see, as it turned out, I got to know the first name of all. He told it me before he died, before I could stop him, with a hand over his mouth. I doubt if there's anyone in the world but me who knows his first name. It's an awful temptation to speak it out loud – introduce it casually into the conversation like you might say by Jove, by George, for Christ's sake. Or whisper it when I think no one's attentive.

'When I was born, time had a different pace to what it has now. Now you walk from one wall to another, and it takes you twenty steps – or twenty miles – who cares? – between the towns. But when I was young we took a leisurely way. Don't bother me with "I must be gone now" or "I've been away so long". I can't talk to you in terms of time – your time and my time are different. Javitt isn't my usual name either even with strangers. It's one I thought up fresh for you, so that you'll have no power at all. I'll change it right away if you escape. I warn you that.

'You get a sense of what I mean when you make love with a girl. The time isn't measured by clocks. Time is fast or slow or it stops for a while altogether. One minute is different to every other minute. When you make love it's a pulse in a man's

44

part which measures time and when you spill yourself there's no time at all. That's how time comes and goes, not by an alarm-clock made by a man with a magnifying glass in his eye. Haven't you ever heard them say, "It's — time" up there?' and he used again the word which I guessed was forbidden like his name, perhaps because it had power too.

'I daresay you are wondering how Maria and me could make a beautiful girl like that one. That's an illusion people have about beauty. Beauty doesn't come from beauty. All that beauty can produce is prettiness. Have you never looked around upstairs and counted the beautiful women with their pretty daughters? Beauty diminishes all the time, it's the law of diminishing returns, and only when you get back to zero, to the real ugly base of things, there's a chance to start again free and independent. Painters who paint what they call ugly things know that. I can still see that little head with its cap of blonde hair coming out from between Maria's thighs and how she leapt out of Maria in a spasm (there wasn't any doctor down here or midwife to give her a name and rob her of power – and she's Miss Ramsgate to you and to the whole world upstairs). Ugliness and beauty; you see it in war too; when there's nothing left of a house but a couple of pillars against the sky, the beauty of it starts all over again like before the builder ruined it. Perhaps when Maria and I go up there next, there'll only be pillars left, sticking up around the flattened world like it was fucking time.' (The word had become familiar to me by this time and no longer had the power to shock.)

'Do you know, boy, that when they make those maps of the universe you are looking at the map of something that looked like that six thousand million years ago? You can't be much more out of date than that, I'll swear. Why, if they've got pictures up there of us taken yesterday, they'll see the world all covered with ice – if their photos are a bit more up to date than ours, that is. Otherwise we won't be there at all, maybe, and it might just as well be a photo of the future. To catch a star while it's alive you have to be as nippy as if you were snatching at a racehorse as it goes by.

'You are a bit scared still of Maria and me because you've never seen anyone like us before. And you'd be scared to see our daughter too, there's no other like her in whatever country she is now, and what good would a scared man be to her? Do you know what a rogue-plant is? And do you know that white cats with blue eyes are deaf? People who keep nursery-gardens look around all the time at the seedlings and they throw away any oddities like weeds. They call them rogues. You won't find many white cats with blue eyes and that's the reason. But sometimes you find someone who wants things different, who's tired of all the plus signs and wants to find zero, and he starts breeding away with the differences. Maria and I are both rogues and we are born of generations of rogues. Do you think I lost this leg in an accident? I was born that way just like Maria with her squawk. Generations of us uglier and uglier, and suddenly out of Maria comes our daughter, who's Miss Ramsgate to you. I don't speak her name even when I'm asleep. We're unique like the Red Grouse. You ask anybody if they can tell you where the Red Grouse came from.

'You are still wondering why we are unique. It's because for generations we haven't been thrown away. Man kills or throws away what he doesn't want. Somebody once in Greece kept the wrong child and exposed the right one, and then one rogue at least was safe and it only needed another. Why, in Tierra del Fuego in starvation years they kill and eat their old women because the dogs are of more value. It's the hardest thing in the world for a rogue to survive. For hundreds of years now we've been living underground and we'll have the laugh of you yet, coming up above for keeps in a dead world. Except I'll bet you your golden po that Miss Ramsgate will be there somewhere – her beauty's rogue too. We have long lives, we – Javitts to you. We've kept our ugliness all those years and why shouldn't she keep her beauty? Like a cat does. A cat is as beautiful the last day as the first. And it keeps its spittle. Not like a dog.

'I can see your eye light up whenever I say Miss Ramsgate, and you still wonder how it comes Maria and I have a child like that in spite of all I'm telling you. Elephants go on breeding till they are ninety years old, don't they, and do you suppose a rogue like Javitt (which isn't my real name) can't go on longer than a beast so stupid it lets itself be harnessed and draw logs? There's another thing we have in common with elephants. No one sees us dead.

'We know the sex-taste of female birds better than we know the sex-taste of women. Only the most beautiful in the hen's eyes survives, so when you admire a peacock you know you have the same taste as a pea-hen. But women are more mysterious than birds. You've heard of beauty and the beast, haven't you? They have rogue-tastes. Just look at me and my leg. You won't find Miss Ramsgate by going round the world preening yourself like a peacock to attract a beautiful woman – she's our daughter and she has rogue-tastes too. She isn't for someone who wants a beautiful wife at his dinner-table to satisfy his vanity, and an understanding wife in bed who'll treat him just the same number of times as he was accustomed to at school – so many times a day or week. She went away, our daughter did, with a want looking for a want – and not a want you can measure in inches either or calculate in numbers by the week. They say that in the northern countries people make love for their health, so it won't be any good looking for her in the north. You might have to go as far as Africa or China. And talking of China . . .'

5

Sometimes I think that I learned more from Javitt – this man who never existed – than from all my schoolmasters. He talked to me while I sat there on the po or lay upon the sacks as no one had ever done before or has ever done since. I could not have expected my mother to take time away from the Fabian pamphlets to say, 'Men are like monkeys – they don't have any season in love, and the monkeys aren't worried by this notion of dying. They tell us from pulpits we're immortal and then they try to frighten us with death. I'm more a monkey than a man. To the monkeys death's an accident. The gorillas don't bury their dead with hearses and crowns of flowers, thinking one day it's going to happen to them and they better put on a show if they want one for themselves too. If one of them dies, it's a special case, and so they can leave it in the ditch. I feel like them. But I'm not a special case yet. I keep clear of hackney-carriages and railway-trains, you won't find horses, wild dogs or machinery down here. I love life and I survive. Up there they talk about natural death, but it's natural death that's unnatural. If we lived for a thousand years – and there's no reason we shouldn't – there'd always be a smash, a bomb, tripping over your left foot – those are the natural deaths. All we need to live is a bit of effort, but nature sows booby-traps in our way.

'Do you believe those skulls monks have in their cells are set there for contemplation? Not on your life. They don't believe in death any more than I do. The skulls are there for the same reason you'll see a queen's portrait in an embassy – they're just part of the official furniture. Do you believe an ambassador ever looks at that face on the wall with a diamond tiara and an empty smile?

'Be disloyal. It's your duty to the human race. The human race needs to survive and it's the loyal man who dies first from anxiety or a bullet or overwork. If you have to earn a living, boy, and the price they make you pay is loyalty, be a double agent – and never let either of the two sides know your real name. The same applies to women and God. They both respect a man they don't own, and they'll go on raising the price they are willing to offer. Didn't Christ say that very thing? Was the prodigal son loyal or the lost shilling or the strayed sheep? The obedient flock didn't give the shepherd any satisfaction or the loyal son interest his father.

'People are afraid of bringing May blossom into the house. They say it's unlucky. The real reason is it smells strong of sex and they are afraid of sex. Why aren't they afraid of fish then, you may rightly ask? Because when they smell fish they smell a holiday ahead and they feel safe from breeding for a short while.'

I remember Javitt's words far more clearly than the passage of time; certainly I must have slept at least twice on the bed of sacks, but I cannot remember Javitt sleeping until the very end – perhaps he slept like a horse or a god, upright. And the broth – that came at regular intervals, so far as I could tell, though there was no sign anywhere of a clock, and once I think they opened for me a tin of sardines from their store (it had a

very Victorian label on it of two bearded sailors and a seal,
but the sardines tasted good).

I think Javitt was glad to have me there. Surely he could not
have been talking quite so amply over the years to Maria who
could only quack in response, and several times he made me
read to him from one of the newspapers. The nearest to our
time I ever found was a local account of the celebrations for
the relief of Mafeking. ('Riots,' Javitt said, 'purge like a dose
of salts.')

Once he told me to pick up the oil-lamp and we would go
for a walk together, and I was able to see how agile he could
be on his one leg. When he stood upright he looked like a
rough carving from a tree-trunk where the sculptor had not
bothered to separate the legs, or perhaps, as with the image on
the cave, they were 'badly executed'. He put one hand on each
wall and hopped gigantically in front of me, and when he
paused to speak (like many old people he seemed unable to
speak and move at the same time) he seemed to be propping
up the whole passage with his arms as thick as pit-beams. At
one point he paused to tell me that we were now directly under
the lake. 'How many tons of water lie up there?' he asked me
– I had never thought of water in tons before that, only in
gallons, but he had the exact figure ready, I can't remember it
now. Further on, where the passage sloped upwards, he paused
again and said, 'Listen,' and I heard a kind of rumbling that
passed overhead and after that a rattling as little cakes of mud
fell around us. 'That's a motor-car,' he said, as an explorer
might have said, 'That's an elephant.'

I asked him whether perhaps there was a way out near there
since we were so close to the surface, and he made his answer,
even to that direct question, ambiguous and general like
a proverb. 'A wise man has only one door to his house,' he
said.

What a boring old man he would have been to an adult
mind, but a child has a hunger to learn which makes him sometimes hang on the lips of the dullest schoolmaster. I thought I
was learning about the world and the universe from Javitt,
and still to this day I wonder how it was that a child could
have invented these details, or have they accumulated year by

year, like coral, in the sea of the unconscious around the original dream?

There were times when he was in a bad humour for no apparent reason, or at any rate for no adequate reason. An example: for all his freedom of speech and range of thought, I found there were tiny rules which had to be obeyed, else the thunder of his invective broke – the way I had to arrange the spoon in the empty broth-bowl, the method of folding a newspaper after it had been read, even the arrangement of my limbs on the bed of sacks.

'I'll cut you off,' he cried once and I pictured him lopping off one of my legs to resemble him. 'I'll starve you, I'll set you alight like a candle for a warning. Haven't I given you a kingdom here of all the treasures of the earth and all the fruits of it, tin by tin, where time can't get in to destroy you and there's no day or night, and you go and defy me with a spoon laid down longways in a saucer? You come of an ungrateful generation.' His arms waved about and cast shadows like wolves on the wall behind the oil-lamp, while Maria sat squatting behind a cylinder of calor-gas in an attitude of terror.

'I haven't even seen your wonderful treasure,' I said with feeble defiance.

'Nor you won't,' he said, 'nor any lawbreaker like you. You lay last night on your back grunting like a small swine, but did I curse you as you deserved? Javitt's patient. He forgives and he forgives seventy times seven, but then you go and lay your spoon longways . . .' He gave a great sigh like a wave withdrawing. He said, 'I forgive even that. There's no fool like an old fool and you will search a long way before you find anything as old as I am – even among the tortoises, the parrots and the elephants. One day I'll show you the treasure, but not now. I'm not in the right mood now. Let time pass. Let time heal.'

I had found the way, however, on an earlier occasion to set him in a good humour and that was to talk to him about his daughter. It came quite easily to me, for I found myself to be passionately in love, as perhaps one can only be at an age when all one wants is to give and the thought of taking is very far removed. I asked him whether he was sad when she left him to go 'upstairs' as he liked to put it.

'I knew it had to come,' he said. 'It was for that she was born. One day she'll be back and the three of us will be together for keeps.'

'Perhaps I'll see her then,' I said.

'You won't live to see that day,' he said, as though it was I who was the old man, not he.

'Do you think she's married?' I asked anxiously.

'She isn't the kind to marry,' he said. 'Didn't I tell you she's a rogue like Maria and me? She has her roots down here. No one marries who has his roots down here.'

'I thought Maria and you were married,' I said anxiously.

He gave a sharp crunching laugh like a nut-cracker closing. 'There's no marrying in the ground,' he said. 'Where would you find the witnesses? Marriage is public. Maria and me, we just grew into each other, that's all, and then she sprouted.'

I sat silent for a long while, brooding on that vegetable picture. Then I said with all the firmness I could muster, 'I'm going to find her when I get out of here.'

'If you get out of here,' he said, 'you'd have to live a very long time and travel a very long way to find her.'

'I'll do just that,' I replied.

He looked at me with a trace of humour. 'You'll have to take a look at Africa,' he said, 'and Asia – and then there's America, North and South, and Australia – you might leave out the Arctic and the other Pole – she was always a warm girl.' And it occurs to me now when I think of the life I have led since, that I have been in most of those regions – except Australia where I have only twice touched down between planes.

'I will go to them all,' I said, 'and I'll find her.' It was as though the purpose of life had suddenly come to me as it must have come often enough to some future explorer when he noticed on a map for the first time an empty space in the heart of a continent.

'You'll need a lot of money,' Javitt jeered at me.

'I'll work my passage,' I said, 'before the mast.' Perhaps it was a reflection of that intention which made the young author W.W. menace his elder brother with such a fate before

51

preserving him for Oxford of all places. The mast was to be a career sacred to me – it was not for George.

'It'll take a long time,' Javitt warned me.

'I'm young,' I said.

I don't know why it is that when I think of this conversation with Javitt the doctor's voice comes back to me saying hopelessly, 'There's always hope.' There's hope perhaps, but there isn't so much time left now as there was then to fulfil a destiny.

That night, when I lay down on the sacks, I had the impression that Javitt had begun to take a favourable view of my case. I woke once in the night and saw him sitting there on what is popularly called a throne, watching me. He closed one eye in a wink and it was like a star going out.

Next morning after my bowl of broth, he suddenly spoke up. 'Today,' he said, 'you are going to see my treasure.'

6

It was a day heavy with the sense of something fateful coming nearer – I call it a day but for all I could have told down there it might have been a night. And I can only compare it in my later experience with those slow hours I have sometimes experienced before I have gone to meet a woman with whom for the first time the act of love is likely to come about. The fuse has been lit, and who can tell the extent of the explosion? A few cups broken or a house in ruins?

For hours Javitt made no further reference to the subject, but after the second cup of broth (or was it perhaps, on that occasion, the tin of sardines?) Maria disappeared behind the screen and when she reappeared she wore a hat. Once, years ago perhaps, it had been a grand hat, a hat for the races, a great black straw affair; now it was full of holes like a colander decorated with one drooping scarlet flower which had been stitched and re-stitched and stitched again. I wondered when I saw her dressed like that whether we were about to go 'upstairs'. But we made no move. Instead she put a kettle upon the stove, warmed a pot and dropped in two spoonfuls of tea. Then she and Javitt sat and watched the kettle like a

52

couple of soothsayers bent over the steaming entrails of a kid, waiting for a revelation. The kettle gave a thin preliminary whine and Javitt nodded and the tea was made. He alone took a cup, sipping it slowly, with his eyes on me, as though he were considering and perhaps revising his decision.

On the edge of his cup, I remember, was a tea-leaf. He took it on his nail and placed it on the back of my hand. I knew very well what that meant. A hard stalk of tea indicated a man upon the way and the soft leaf a woman; this was a soft leaf. I began to strike it with the palm of my other hand counting as I did so, 'One, two, three.' It lay flat, adhering to my hand. 'Four, five.' It was on my fingers now and I said, triumphantly, 'In five days,' thinking of Javitt's daughter in the world above.

Javitt shook his head. 'You don't count time like that with us,' he said. 'That's five decades of years.' I accepted his correction – he must know his own country best, and it's only now that I find myself calculating, if every day down there were ten years long, what age in our reckoning could Javitt have claimed?

I have no idea what he had learned from the ceremony of the tea, but at least he seemed satisfied. He rose on his one leg, and now that he had his arms stretched out to either wall, he reminded me of a gigantic crucifix, and the crucifix moved in great hops down the way we had taken the day before. Maria gave me a little push from behind and I followed. The oil lamp in Maria's hand cast long shadows ahead of us.

First we came under the lake and I remembered the tons of water hanging over us like a frozen falls, and after that we reached the spot where we had halted before, and again a car went rumbling past on the road above. But this time we continued our shuffling march. I calculated that now we had crossed the road which led to Winton Halt; we must be somewhere under the inn called The Three Keys, which was kept by our gardener's uncle, and after that we should have arrived below the Long Mead, a field with a small minnowy stream along its northern border owned by a farmer called Howell. I had not given up all idea of escape and I noted our route carefully and the distance we had gone. I had hoped for some side-passage which might indicate that there was another entrance to the tunnel, but there seemed to be none and I was disappointed to find that before we travelled below the inn we descended quite steeply, perhaps in order to avoid the cellars – indeed at one moment I heard a groaning and a turbulence as though the gardener's uncle were taking delivery of some new barrels of beer.

We must have gone nearly half a mile before the passage came to an end in a kind of egg-shaped hall. Facing us was a kitchen-dresser of unstained wood, very similar to the one in which my mother kept her stores of jam, sultanas, raisins and the like.

'Open up, Maria,' Javitt said, and Maria shuffled by me, clanking a bunch of keys and quacking with excitement, while the lamp swung to and fro like a censer.

'She's heated up,' Javitt said. 'It's many days since she saw the treasure last.' I do not know which kind of time he was referring to then, but judging from her excitement I think the days must really have represented decades – she had even forgotten which key fitted the lock and she tried them all and failed and tried again before the tumbler turned.

I was disappointed when I first saw the interior – I had expected gold bricks and a flow of Maria Theresa dollars spilling on the floor, and there were only a lot of shabby cardboard-boxes on the upper shelves and the lower shelves were empty. I think Javitt noted my disappointment and was stung by it. 'I told you,' he said, 'the moit's down below for safety.' But I wasn't to stay disappointed very long. He took down one of the biggest boxes off the top shelf and shook the contents on to the earth at my feet, as though defying me to belittle *that*.

And *that* was a sparkling mass of jewellery such as I had never seen before – I was going to say in all the colours of the rainbow, but the colours of stones have not that pale girlish simplicity. There were reds almost as deep as raw liver, stormy blues, greens like the underside of a wave, yellow sunset colours, greys like a shadow on snow, and stones without colour at all that sparkled brighter than all the rest. I say I'd seen nothing like it: it is the scepticism of middle-age which leads me now to compare that treasure-trove with the caskets overflowing with artificial jewellery which you sometimes see in the shop-windows of Italian tourist-resorts.

And there again I find myself adjusting a dream to the kind of criticism I ought to reserve for some agent's report on the import or export value of coloured glass. If this was a dream, these were real stones. Absolute reality belongs to dreams and not to life. The gold of dreams is not the diluted gold of even the best goldsmith, there are no diamonds in dreams made of paste – what seems is. 'Who seems most kingly is the king.'

I went down on my knees and bathed my hands in the treasure, and while I knelt there Javitt opened box after box and poured the contents upon the ground. There is no avarice in a child. I didn't concern myself with the value of this horde: it was simply a treasure, and a treasure is to be valued for its own sake and not for what it will buy. It was only years later, after a deal of literature and learning and knowledge at second hand, that W.W. wrote of the treasure as something with which he could save the family fortunes. I was nearer to the jackdaw in my dream, caring only for the glitter and the sparkle.

'It's nothing to what lies below out of sight,' Javitt remarked with pride.

There were necklaces and bracelets, lockets and bangles, pins and rings and pendants and buttons. There were quantities of those little gold objects which girls like to hang on their bracelets: the Vendôme column and the Eiffel Tower and a Lion of St Mark's, a champagne bottle and a tiny booklet with leaves of gold inscribed with the names of places important perhaps to a pair of lovers – Paris, Brighton, Rome, Assisi and Moreton-in-Marsh. There were gold coins too – some with the heads of Roman emperors and others of Victoria and George IV and Frederick Barbarossa. There were birds made out of precious stone with diamond-eyes, and buckles for shoes and belts, hairpins too with the rubies turned into roses, and vinaigrettes. There were toothpicks of gold, and swizzlesticks, and little spoons to dig the wax out of your ears of gold too, and cigarette-holders studded with diamonds, and small boxes of gold for pastilles and snuff, horse-shoes for

the ties of hunting men, and emerald-hounds for the lapels
of hunting women: fishes were there too and little carrots of
ruby for luck, diamond-stars which had perhaps decorated
generals or statesmen, golden key-rings with emerald-initials,
and sea-shells picked out with pearls, and a portrait of a
dancing-girl in gold and enamel, with Haidee inscribed in what
I suppose were rubies.

'Enough's enough,' Javitt said, and I had to drag myself
away, as it seemed to me, from all the riches of the world, its
pursuits and enjoyments. Maria would have packed everything that lay there back into the cardboard-boxes, but Javitt
said with his lordliest voice, 'Let them lie,' and back we went
in silence the way we had come, in the same order, our
shadows going ahead. It was as if the sight of the treasure had
exhausted me. I lay down on the sacks without waiting for my
broth and fell at once asleep. In my dream within a dream
somebody laughed and wept.

7

I have said that I can't remember how many days and nights
I spent below the garden. The number of times I slept is really
no guide, for I slept simply when I had the inclination or when
Javitt commanded me to lie down, there being no light or
darkness save what the oil-lamp determined, but I am almost
sure it was after this sleep of exhaustion that I woke with the
full intention somehow to reach home again. Up till now I
had acquiesced in my captivity with little complaint; perhaps
the meals of broth were palling on me, though I doubt if that
was the reason, for I have fed for longer, with as little variety
and less appetite, in Africa; perhaps the sight of Javitt's treasure had been a climax which robbed my story of any further
interest; perhaps, and I think this is the most likely reason, I
wanted to begin my search for Miss Ramsgate.

Whatever the motive, I came awake determined from my
deep sleep, as suddenly as I had fallen into it. The wick was
burning low in the oil-lamp and I could hardly distinguish
Javitt's features and Maria was out of sight somewhere behind
the curtain. To my astonishment Javitt's eyes were closed – it
had never occurred to me before that there were moments

when these two might sleep. Very quietly, with my eyes on Javitt, I slipped off my shoes – it was now or never. When I had got them off with less sound than a mouse makes, an idea came to me and I withdrew the laces – I can still hear the sharp ting of the metal tag ringing on the gold po beside my sacks. I thought I had been too clever by half, for Javitt stirred – but then he was still again and I slipped off my makeshift bed and crawled over to him where he sat on the lavatory-seat. I knew that, unfamiliar as I was with the tunnel, I could never outpace Javitt, but I was taken aback when I realized that it was impossible to bind together the ankles of a one-legged man.

But neither could a one-legged man travel without the help of his hands – the hands which lay now conveniently folded like a statue's on his lap. One of the things my brother had taught me was to make a slip-knot. I made one now with the laces joined and very gently, millimetre by millimetre, passed it over Javitt's hands and wrists, then pulled it tight.

I had expected him to wake with a howl of rage and even in my fear felt some of the pride Jack must have experienced at outwitting the giant. I was ready to flee at once, taking the lamp with me, but his very silence detained me. He only opened one eye, so that again I had the impression that he was winking at me. He tried to move his hands, felt the knot, and then acquiesced in their imprisonment. I expected him to call for Maria, but he did nothing of the kind, just watching me with his one open eye.

Suddenly I felt ashamed of myself. 'I'm sorry,' I said.

'Ha, ha,' he said, 'my prodigal, the strayed sheep, you're learning fast.'

'I promise not to tell a soul.'

'They wouldn't believe you if you did,' he said.

'I'll be going now,' I whispered with regret, lingering there absurdly, as though with half of myself I would have been content to stay for always.

'You better,' he said. 'Maria might have different views from me.' He tried his hands again. 'You tie a good knot.'

'I'm going to find your daughter,' I said, 'whatever you may think.'

'Good luck to you then,' Javitt said. 'You'll have to travel

57

a long way; you'll have to forget all your schoolmasters try to teach you; you must lie like a horse-trader and not be tied up with loyalties any more than you are here, and who knows? I doubt it, but you might, you just might.'

I turned away to take the lamp, and then he spoke again. 'Take your golden po as a souvenir,' he said. 'Tell them you found it in an old cupboard. You've got to have something when you start a search to give you substance.'

'Thank you,' I said, 'I will. You've been very kind.' I began – absurdly in view of his bound wrists – to hold out my hand like a departing guest; then I stooped to pick up the po just as Maria, woken perhaps by our voices, came through the curtain. She took the situation in as quick as a breath and squawked at me – what I don't know – and made a dive with her bird-like hand.

I had the start of her down the passage and the advantage of the light, and I was a few feet ahead when I reached Camp Indecision, but at that point, what with the wind of my passage and the failing wick, the lamp went out. I dropped it on the earth and groped on in the dark. I could hear the scratch and whimper of Maria's sequin dress, and my nerves leapt when her feet set the lamp rolling on my tracks. I don't remember much after that. Soon I was crawling upwards, making better speed on my knees than she could do in her skirt, and a little later I saw a grey light where the roots of the tree parted. When I came up into the open it was much the same early morning hour as the one when I had entered the cave. I could hear kwahk, kwahk, kwahk, come up from below the ground – I don't know if it was a curse or a menace or just a farewell, but for many nights afterwards I lay in bed afraid that the door would open and Maria would come in to fetch me, when the house was silent and asleep. Yet strangely enough I felt no fear of Javitt, then or later.

Perhaps – I can't remember – I dropped the gold po at the entrance of the tunnel as a propitiation to Maria; certainly I didn't have it with me when I rafted across the lake or when Joe, our dog, came leaping out of the house at me and sent me sprawling on my back in the dew of the lawn by the green broken fountain.

PART THREE

1

Wilditch stopped writing and looked up from the paper. The night had passed and with it the rain and the wet wind. Out of the window he could see thin rivers of blue sky winding between the banks of cloud, and the sun as it slanted in gleamed weakly on the cap of his pen. He read the last sentence which he had written and saw how again at the end of his account he had described his adventure as though it were one which had really happened and not something that he had dreamed during the course of a night's truancy or invented a few years later for the school-magazine. Somebody, early though it was, trundled a wheelbarrow down the gravel-path beyond the fountain. The sound, like the dream, belonged to childhood.

He went downstairs and unlocked the front door. There unchanged was the broken fountain and the path which led to the Dark Walk, and he was hardly surprised when he saw Ernest, his uncle's gardener, coming towards him behind the wheelbarrow. Ernest must have been a young man in the days of the dream and he was an old man now, but to a child a man in the twenties approaches middle-age and so he seemed much as Wilditch remembered him. There was something of Javitt about him, though he had a big moustache and not a beard – perhaps it was only a brooding and scrutinizing look and that air of authority and possession which had angered Mrs Wilditch when she approached him for vegetables.

'Why, Ernest,' Wilditch said, 'I thought you had retired?'

Ernest put down the handle of the wheelbarrow and regarded Wilditch with reserve. 'It's Master William, isn't it?'

'Yes. George said –'

'Master George was right in a way, but I have to lend a hand still. There's things in this garden others don't know about.' Perhaps he *had* been the model for Javitt, for there

59

was something in his way of speech that suggested the same ambiguity.

'Such as . . .?'

'It's not everyone can grow asparagus in chalky soil,' he said, making a general statement out of the particular in the same way Javitt had done. 'You've been away a long time, Master William.'

'I've travelled a lot.'

'We heard one time you was in Africa and another time in Chinese parts. Do you like a black skin, Master William?'

'I suppose at one time or another I've been fond of a black skin.'

'I wouldn't have thought they'd win a beauty prize,' Ernest said.

'Do you know Ramsgate, Ernest?'

'A gardener travels far enough in a day's work,' he said. The wheelbarrow was full of fallen leaves after the night's storm. 'Are the Chinese as yellow as people say?'

'No.'

There *was* a difference, Wilditch thought: Javitt never asked for information, he gave it: the weight of water, the age of the earth, the sexual habits of a monkey. 'Are there many changes in the garden,' he asked, 'since I was here?'

'You'll have heard the pasture was sold?'

'Yes. I was thinking of taking a walk before breakfast – down the Dark Walk perhaps to the lake and the island.'

'Ah.'

'Did you ever hear any story of a tunnel under the lake?'

'There's no tunnel there. For what would there be a tunnel?'

'No reason that I know. I suppose it was something I dreamed.'

'As a boy you was always fond of that island. Used to hide there from the missus.'

'Do you remember a time when I ran away?'

'You was always running away. The missus used to tell me to go and find you. I'd say to her right out, straight as I'm talking to you, I've got enough to do digging the potatoes you are always asking for. I've never known a woman get through potatoes like she did. You'd have thought she ate them. She could have been living on potatoes and not on the fat of the land.'

'Do you think I was treasure-hunting? Boys do.'

'You was hunting for something. That's what I said to the folk round here when you were away in those savage parts – not even coming back here for your uncle's funeral. "You take my word," I said to them, "he hasn't changed, he's off hunting for something, like he always did, though I doubt if he knows what he's after," I said to them. "The next we hear," I said, "he'll be standing on his head in Australia." '

Wilditch remarked with regret, 'Somehow I never looked there'; he was surprised that he had spoken aloud. 'And The Three Keys, is it still in existence?'

'Oh, it's there all right, but the brewers bought it when my uncle died and it's not a free house any more.'

'Did they alter it much?'

'You'd hardly know it was the same house with all the pipes and tubes. They put in what they call pressure, so you can't get an honest bit of beer without a bubble in it. My uncle was content to go down to the cellar for a barrel, but it's all machinery now.'

'When they made all those changes you didn't hear any talk of a tunnel under the cellar?'

'Tunnel again. What's got you thinking of tunnels? The only tunnel I know is the railway tunnel at Bugham and that's five miles off.'

'Well, I'll be walking on, Ernest, or it will be breakfast time before I've seen the garden.'

'And I suppose now you'll be off again to foreign parts. What's it to be this time? Australia?'

'It's too late for Australia now.'

Ernest shook his brindled head at Wilditch with an air of sober disapproval. 'When I was born,' he said, 'time had a different pace to what it seems to have now,' and, lifting the handle of the wheelbarrow, he was on his way towards the new iron gate before Wilditch had time to realize he had used almost the very words of Javitt. The world was the world he knew.

2

The Dark Walk was small and not very dark – perhaps the laurels had thinned with the passing of time, but the cobwebs were there as in his childhood to brush his face as he went by. At the end of the walk there was the wooden gate on to the green which had always in his day been locked – he had never known why that route out of the garden was forbidden him, but he had discovered a way of opening the gate with the rim of a halfpenny. Now he could find no halfpennies in his pocket.

When he saw the lake he realized how right George had been. It was only a small pond, and a few feet from the margin there was an island the size of the room in which last night they had dined. There *were* a few bushes growing there, and even a few trees, one taller and larger than the others, but certainly it was neither the sentinel-pine of W.W.'s story nor the great oak of his memory. He took a few steps back from the margin of the pond and jumped.

He hadn't quite made the island, but the water in which he landed was only a few inches deep. Was any of the water deep enough to float a raft? He doubted it. He sloshed ashore, the water not even penetrating his shoes. So this little spot of earth had contained Camp Hope and Friday's Cave. He wished that he had the cynicism to laugh at the half-expectation which had brought him to the island.

The bushes came only to his waist and he easily pushed through them towards the largest tree. It was difficult to believe that even a small child could have been lost here. He was in the world that George saw every day, making his round of a not very remarkable garden. For perhaps a minute, as he pushed his way through the bushes, it seemed to him that his whole life had been wasted, much as a man who has been betrayed by a woman wipes out of his mind even the happy years with her. If it had not been for his dream of the tunnel and the bearded man and the hidden treasure, couldn't he have made a less restless life for himself, as George in fact had done, with marriage, children, a home? He tried to persuade

himself that he was exaggerating the importance of a dream.
His lot had probably been decided months before that when
George was reading him *The Romance of Australian Exploration*. If a child's experience does really form his future life,
surely he had been formed, not by Javitt, but by Grey and
Burke. It was his pride that at least he had never taken his
various professions seriously: he had been loyal to no one –
not even to the girl in Africa (Javitt would have approved
his disloyalty). Now he stood beside the ignoble tree that had
no roots above the ground which could possibly have formed
the entrance to a cave and he looked back at the house: it
was so close that he could see George at the window of the
bathroom lathering his face. Soon the bell would be going
for breakfast and they would be sitting opposite each other
exchanging the morning small talk. There was a good train
back to London at 10.25. He supposed that it was the effect
of his disease that he was so tired – not sleepy but achingly
tired as though at the end of a long journey.

After he had pushed his way a few feet through the bushes
he came on the blackened remains of an oak; it had been
split by lightning probably and then sawed close to the ground
for logs. It could easily have been the source of his dream.
He tripped on the old roots hidden in the grass, and squatting
down on the ground he laid his ear close to the earth. He had
an absurd desire to hear from somewhere far below the
kwahk, kwahk from a roofless mouth and the deep rumbling
of Javitt's voice saying, 'We are hairless, you and I,' shaking
his beard at him, 'so's the hippopotamus and the elephant
and the dugong – you wouldn't know, I suppose, what a
dugong is. We survive the longest, the hairless ones.'

But, of course, he could hear nothing except the emptiness
you hear when a telephone rings in an empty house. Something tickled his ear, and he almost hoped to find a sequin
which had survived the years under the grass, but it was only
an ant staggering with a load towards its tunnel.

Wilditch got to his feet. As he levered himself upright, his
hand was scraped by the sharp rim of some metal object in
the earth. He kicked the object free and found it was an old
tin chamber-pot. It had lost all colour in the ground except

that inside the handle there adhered a few flakes of yellow paint.

3

How long he had been sitting there with the pot between his knees he could not tell; the house was out of sight: he was as small now as he had been then – he couldn't see over the tops of the bushes, and he was back in Javitt's time. He turned the pot over and over; it was certainly not a golden po, but that proved nothing either way; a child might have mistaken it for one when it was newly painted. Had he then really dropped this in his flight – which meant that somewhere underneath him now Javitt sat on his lavatory-seat and Maria quacked beside the calor-gas ... ? There was no certainty; perhaps years ago, when the paint was fresh, he had discovered the pot, just as he had done this day, and founded a whole afternoon-legend around it. Then why had W.W. omitted it from his story?

Wilditch shook the loose earth out of the po, and it rang on a pebble just as it had rung against the tag of his shoelace fifty years ago. He had a sense that there was a decision he had to make all over again. Curiosity was growing inside him like the cancer. Across the pond the bell rang for breakfast and he thought, 'Poor mother – she had reason to fear,' turning the tin chamber-pot on his lap.

A VISIT TO MORIN

1

Le Diable au Ciel – there it was on a shelf in the Colmar bookshop causing a memory to reach out to me from the past of twenty years ago. One didn't often, in the 1950s, see Pierre Morin's novels on display, and yet here were two copies of his once famous book, and looking along the rows of paper-bindings I discovered others, as though there existed in Alsace a secret *cave*, like those hidden cellars where wines were once preserved from the enemy for the days when peace would return.

I had admired Pierre Morin when I was a boy, but I had almost forgotten him. He was even then an older writer on the point of abandonment by his public, but the language-class in an English public school is always a long way behind the Paris fashions. We happened at Collingworth to have a Roman Catholic master who belonged to the generation which Morin had pleased or offended. He had offended the orthodox Catholics in his own country and pleased the liberal Catholics abroad; he had pleased, too, the Protestants who believed in God with the same intensity that he seemed to show, and he used to find enthusiastic readers among non-Christians who, when once they had accepted imaginatively his premises, perhaps detected in his work the freedom of speculation which put his fellow Catholics on their guard. How fresh and exciting his work had appeared to my school-master's generation; and to me, brought up in a lower form on *Les Misérables* and the poems of Lamartine, he was a re-volutionary writer. But it is the fate of revolutionaries that the world accepts them. The excitement has gone from Morin's pages. Only the orthodox read him now, when the whole world seems prepared to believe in a god, except strangely enough – but I will not anticipate the point of my small anecdote which may yet provide a footnote to the literary history of Morin's day. When I publish it no harm can be done. Morin will be dead in the flesh as well as being

dead as a writer, and he has left, so far as I am aware, no
descendants and no disciples.

I yet recall with pleasure those French classes presided
over by a Mr Strangeways from Chile; his swarthy complexion
was said by his enemies to indicate Spanish blood (it was the
period of the Spanish Civil War when anything Spanish and
Roman was regarded as Fascist) and by his friends, of whom
I was one, a dash of Indian. In dull fact his father was an en-
gineer from Wolverhampton and his mother came from
Louisiana and was only Latin after three removes. At these
senior classes we no longer studied syntax – at which Mr
Strangeways was in any case weak. Mr Strangeways read
aloud to us and we read aloud to him, but after five minutes
we would launch into literary criticism, pulling to pieces with
youthful daring – Mr Strangeways like so many schoolmasters
remained always youthful – the great established names and
building up with exaggerated appreciation those who had not
yet 'arrived'. Of course Morin had arrived years before, but
of that we were unaware in our brick prison five hundred
miles from the Seine – he hadn't reached the school text-
books; he hadn't yet been mummified by Messrs Hachette et
Cie. Where we didn't understand his meaning, there were no
editor's notes to kill speculation.

'Can he really believe that?' I remember exclaiming to Mr
Strangeways when a character in *Le Diable au Ciel* made
some dark and horrifying statement on the Atonement or
the Redemption, and I remember Mr Strangeways' blunt
reply, flapping the sleeves of his short black gown, 'But I
believe it too, Dunlop.' He did not leave it at that or allow
himself to get involved in a theological debate, which might
have imperilled his post in my Protestant school. He went on
to indicate that we were unconcerned with what the author
believed. The author had chosen as his viewpoint the character of an orthodox Catholic – all his thoughts therefore must
be affected, as they would be in life, by his orthodoxy. Morin's
technique forbade him to play a part in the story himself;
even to show irony would be to cheat, though perhaps we
might detect something of Morin's view from the fact that
the orthodoxy of Durobier was extended to the furthest

possible limits, so that at the close of the book we had the impression of a man stranded on a long strip of sand from which there was no possibility of advance, and to retreat towards the shore would be to surrender. 'Is this true or is it not true?' His whole creed was concerned in the answer.

'You mean,' I asked Mr Strangeways, 'that perhaps Morin does not believe?'

'I mean nothing of the kind. No one has seriously questioned his Catholicism, only his prudence. Anyway that's not true criticism. A novel is made up of words and characters. Are the words well chosen and do the characters live? All the rest belongs to literary gossip. You are not in this class to learn how to be gossip-writers.'

And yet in those days I would have liked to know. Sometimes Mr Strangeways, recognizing my interest in Morin, would lend me Roman Catholic literary periodicals which contained notices of the novelist's work that often offended his principle of leaving the author's views out of account. I found Morin was sometimes accused of Jansenism – whatever that might be: others called him an Augustinian – a name which meant as little to me – and in the better printed and bulkier reviews I thought I detected a note of grievance. He believed all the right things, they could find no specific fault, and yet ... it was as though some of his characters accepted a dogma so wholeheartedly that they drew out its implications to the verge of absurdity, while others examined a dogma as though they were constitutional lawyers determined on confining it to a kind of legal minimum. Durobier, I am sure, would have staked his life on a literal Assumption: at some point in history, somewhere in the latter years of the first century A.D., the body of the Virgin had floated skywards, leaving an empty tomb. On the other hand there was a character called Sagrin, in one of the minor novels, perhaps *Le Bien Pensant*, who believed that the holy body had rotted in the grave like other bodies. The strange thing was that both views seemed to possess irritating qualities to Catholic reviewers, and yet both proved to be equally in accordance with the dogmatic pronouncement when it came. One could assert therefore that they were orthodox; yet the orthodox critics seemed to scent heresy like a rat dead somewhere under the boards, at a spot they could not locate.

These, of course, were ancient criticisms, fished out of Mr Strangeways' cupboard, full of old French magazines dating back to his long-lost sojourn in Paris some time during the late 'twenties, when he had attended lectures at the Sorbonne and drunk beer at the Dôme. The word 'paradox' was frequently used with an air of disapproval. Perhaps after all the orthodox were proved right, for I certainly was to discover just how far Morin carried in his own life the sense of paradox.

2

I am not one of those who revisit their old school, or what a disappointment I would have proved to Mr Strangeways, who must by now be on the point of retirement. I think he had pictured me in the future as a distinguished writer for the weeklies on the subject of French literature – perhaps even as the author of a scholarly biography of Corneille. In fact, after an undistinguished war-record, I obtained a post, with the help of influential connexions, in a firm of wine-merchants. My French syntax, so neglected by Mr Strangeways, had been improved by the war and proved useful to the firm, and I suppose I had a certain literary flair which enabled me to improve on the rather old-fashioned style of the catalogues. The directors had been content for too long with the jargon of the Wine Society – 'An unimportant but highly sympathetic wine for light occasions among friends.' I introduced a more realistic note and substituted knowledge for knowingness. 'This wine comes from a small vineyard on the western slopes of the Mont Soleil range. The soil in this region has Jurassic elements, as the vineyard is on the edge of the great Jurassic fissure which extends across Europe from the Urals, and this encourages the cultivation of a small, strong, dark grape with a high sugar-content, less vulnerable than more famous wines to the chances of weather.' Of course it was the same 'unimportant' wine, but my description gave the host material for his vanity.

Business had brought me to Colmar – we had found it

necessary to change our agent there, and as I am a single man
and find the lonely Christmases of London sad and regretful,
I had chosen to combine my visit with the Christmas holiday.
One does not feel alone abroad; I imagined drinking my way
through the festival itself in some *bierhaus* decorated with
holly, myself invisible behind the fumes of cigars. A German
Christmas is Christmas *par excellence*: singing, sentiment,
gluttony.

I said to the shop assistant, 'You seem to have a good supply
of M. Morin's books.'

'He is very popular,' she said.

'I got the impression that in Paris he is no longer much
read.'

'We are Catholics here,' she said with a note of reproof.
'Besides, he lives near Colmar, and we are very proud he chose
to settle in our neighbourhood.'

'How long has he been here?'

'He came immediately after the war. We consider him
almost one of us. We have all his books in German also – you
will see them over there. Some of us feel he is even finer in
German than in French. German,' she said, scrutinizing me
with contempt as I picked up a French edition of *Le Diable
au Ciel,* 'has a better vocabulary for the profundities.'

I told her I had admired M. Morin's novels since my school-
days. She softened towards me then, and I left the shop with
M. Morin's address – a village fifteen miles from Colmar. I
was uncertain all the same whether I would call on him. What
really had I to say to him to excuse the vulgarity of my
curiosity? Writing is the most private of all the arts, and yet
few of us hesitate to invade the writer's home. We have all
heard of that one caller from Porlock, but hundreds of callers
every day are ringing door-bells, lifting receivers, thrusting
themselves into the secret room where a writer works and
lives.

I doubt whether I should have ventured to ring M. Morin's
bell, but I caught sight of him two days later at the Midnight
Mass in a village outside Colmar; it was not the village where
I had been told he lived, and I wondered why he had come
such a distance alone. Midnight Mass is a service which even

a non-believer like myself finds inexplicably moving. Perhaps there is some memory of childhood which makes the journey through the darkness, the lighted windows and the frosty night, the slow gathering of silent strangers from the four quarters of the countryside moving and significant. There was a crib to the left of the door as I came in – the plaster-baby sprawled in the plaster-lap, and the cows, the sheep and the shepherd cast long shadows in the candlelight. Among the kneeling women was an old man whose face I seemed to remember: a round head like a peasant's, the skin wrinkled like a stale apple, with the hair gone from the crown. He knelt, bowed his head, and rose again. There had just been time, I suppose, for a formal prayer, but it must have been a short one. His chin was stubbled white like the field outside, and there was so little about him to suggest a member of the French Academy that I might have taken him for the peasant he appeared to be, in his suit of respectable and shiny black and his black tie like a bootlace, if I had not been attracted by the eyes. The eyes gave him away: they seemed to know too much and to have seen further than the season and the fields. Of a very clear pale blue, they continually shifted focus, looking close and looking away, observant, sad and curious like those of a man caught in some great catastrophe which it is his duty to record, but which he cannot bear to contemplate for any length of time. It was not, of course, during his short prayer before the crib that I had time to watch Morin so closely; but when the congregation was shuffling up towards the altar for Communion, Morin and I found ourselves alone among the empty chairs. It was then I recognized him – perhaps from memories of old photographs in Mr Strangeways' reviews, I do not know; yet I was convinced of his identity, and I wondered what it was that kept this old distinguished Catholic from going up with the others, at this Mass of all Masses in the year, to receive the Sacrament. Had he perhaps inadvertently broken his fast, or was he a man who suffered from scruples and did he believe that he had been guilty of some act of uncharity or greed? There could not be many serious temptations, I thought, for a man who must be approaching his eightieth year. And yet I would not have

believed him to be scrupulous; it was from his own novels I
had learnt of the existence of this malady of the religious,
and I would never have supposed the creator of Durobier to
have suffered from the same disease as his character. However, a novelist may sometimes write most objectively of his
own failings.

We sat there alone at the back of the church. The air was
as cold and still as a frozen tree and the candles burned
straight on the altar and God, so they believed, passed along
the altar-rail. This was the birth of Christianity: outside in
the dark was old savage Judea, but in here the world was only
a few minutes old. It was the Year One again, and I felt the
old sentimental longing to believe as those, I suppose, believed
who came back one by one from the rail, with lips set like
closed doors around the dissolving wafer and with crossed
hands. If I had said to one of them, 'Teach me why you believe,' what would the answer have been? I thought perhaps I
knew, for once in the war – driven by fear and disgust at the
sight of the dead – I had spoken to a Catholic chaplain in just
that way. He didn't belong to my unit, he was a busy man – it
isn't the job of a chaplain in the line to instruct or convert
and he was not to blame that he could convey nothing of his
faith to an outsider like myself. He lent me two books – one
a penny-catechism with its catalogue of preposterous questions and answers, smug and explanatory: mystery like a
butterfly killed by cyanide, stiffened and laid out with pins and
paper-strips; the other a sober enough study of gospel dates.
I lost them both in a few days, with three bottles of whisky,
my jeep and the corporal whose name I had not had time to
learn before he was killed, while I was peeing in the green
canal close by. I don't suppose I'd have kept the books much
longer anyway. They were not the kind of help I needed,
nor was the chaplain the man to give it me. I remember asking him if he had read Morin's novels. 'I haven't time to waste
with him,' he said abruptly.

'They were the first books,' I said, 'to interest me in your
faith.'

'You'd have done much better to read Chesterton,' he said.

So it was odd to find myself there at the back of the church witn Morin himself. He was the first to leave and I followed him out. I was glad to go, for the sentimental attraction of a Midnight Mass was lost in the long ennui of the Communions.

'M. Morin,' I said in that low voice we assume in a church or hospital.

He looked quickly, and I thought defensively, up.

I said, 'Forgive my speaking to you like this, M. Morin, but your books have given me such great pleasure.' Had the man from Porlock employed the same banal phrases?

'You are English?' he asked.

'Yes.'

He spoke to me then in English. 'You write yourself? Forgive my asking, but I do not know your name.'

'Dunlop. But I don't write. I buy and sell wine.'

'A profession more worthy of respect,' M. Morin said. 'If you would care to drive with me – I live only ten kilometres from here – I think I could show you a wine you may not have encountered.'

'Surely, it's rather late, M. Morin. And I have a driver ...'

'Send him home. After Midnight Mass I find it difficult to sleep. You would be doing me a kindness.' When I hesitated he said, 'As for tomorrow, that is just any day of the year, and I don't like visitors.'

I tried to make a joke of it. 'You mean it's my only chance?' and he replied 'Yes' with seriousness. The doors of the church swung open and the congregation came slowly out into the frosty glitter, pecking at the holy water stoup with their forefingers, chatting cheerfully again as the mystery receded, greeting neighbours. A wailing child marked the lateness of the hour like a clock. M. Morin strode away and I followed him.

3

M. Morin drove with clumsy violence, wrenching at his gears, scraping the right-hand hedgerows as though the car were a new invention and he a courageous pioneer in its use. 'So you have read some of my books?' he asked.

'A great many, when I was a schoolboy ...'

'You mean they are fit only for children?'

72

'I mean nothing of the sort.'

'What can a child find in them?'

'I was sixteen when I began to read them. That's not a child.'

'Oh well, now they are only read by the old – and the pious. Are you pious, Mr Dunlop?'

'I'm not a Catholic.'

'I'm glad to hear that. Then I shan't offend you.'

'Once I thought of becoming one.'

'Second thoughts are best.'

'I think it was your books that made me curious.'

'I will not take responsibility,' he said. 'I am not a theologian.' We bumped over a little branch railway-track without altering speed and swerved right through a gateway much in need of repair. A light hanging in a porch shone on an open door.

'Don't you lock up,' I asked him, 'in these parts?'

He said, 'Ten years ago – times were bad then – a hungry man was frozen to death near here on Christmas morning. He could find no one to open a door: there was a blizzard, but they were all at church. Come in,' he said angrily from the porch; 'are you looking round, making notes of how I live? Have you deceived me? Are you a journalist?'

If I had had my own car with me I would have driven away. 'M. Morin,' I said, 'there are different kinds of hunger. You seem only to cater for one kind.' He went ahead of me into a small study – a desk, a table, two comfortable chairs, and some bookshelves oddly bare – I could see no sign of his own books. There was a bottle of brandy on the table, ready perhaps for the stranger and the blizzard that would never again come together in this place.

'Sit down,' he said, 'sit down. You must forgive me if I was discourteous. I am unused to company. I will go and find the wine I spoke of. Make yourself at home.' I had never seen a man less at home himself. It was as if he were camping in a house that belonged to another.

While he was away, I looked more closely at his bookshelves. He had not re-bound any of his paper-backs and his shelves had the appearance of bankrupt stock: small tears and dust and the discoloration of sunlight. There was a great deal of theology, some poetry, very few novels. He came back with the wine and a plate of salami. When he had tasted the wine himself, he poured me a glass. 'It will do,' he said.

'It's excellent. Remarkable.'

'A small vineyard twenty miles away. I will give you the address before you go. For me, on a night like this, I prefer brandy.' So perhaps it was really for himself and not for the stranger, I thought, that the bottle stood ready.

'It's certainly cold.'

'It was not the weather I meant.'

'I have been looking at your library. You read a lot of theology.'

'Not now.'

'I wonder if you would recommend . . .' But I had even less success with him than with the chaplain.

'No. Not if you want to believe. If you are foolish enough to want that you must avoid theology.'

'I don't understand.'

He said, 'A man can accept anything to do with God until scholars begin to go into the details and the implications. A man can accept the Trinity, but the arguments that follow . . .' He gave a gesture of rejection. 'I would never try to determine some point in differential calculus with a two-times-two table. You end by disbelieving the calculus.' He poured out two more glasses and drank his as though it were vodka. 'I used to believe in Revelation, but I never believed in the capacity of the human mind.'

'You used to believe?'

'Yes, Mr Dunlop – was that the name? – *used*. If you are one of those who come seeking belief, go away. You won't find it here.'

'But from your books . . .'

'You will find none of them,' he said, 'on my shelves.'

'I noticed you have some theology.'

'Even disbelief,' he said, with his eye on the brandy bottle, 'needs bolstering somehow.' I noticed that the brandy very quickly affected him, not only his readiness to communicate with me, but even the physical appearance of his eyeballs. It was as if the little blood-cells had been waiting under the white membrane to burst at once like buds with the third glass. He said, 'Can you find anything more inadequate than the scholastic arguments for the existence of God?'

'I'm afraid I don't know them.'

'The arguments from an agent, from a cause?'

'No.'

'They tell you that in all change there are two elements, that which is changed and that which changes it. Each agent of change is itself determined by some higher agent. Can this go on *ad infinitum*? Oh no, they say, that would not give the finality that thought demands. But does thought demand it? Why shouldn't the chain go on for ever? Man has invented the idea of infinity. In any case how trivial any argument based on what human thought demands must be. The thoughts of you and me and Monsieur Dupont. I would prefer the thoughts of an ape. Its instincts are less corrupted. Show me a gorilla praying and I might believe again.'

'But surely there are other arguments?'

'Four. Each more inadequate than the other. It needs a child to say to these theologians, Why? Why not? Why not an infinite series of causes? Why should the existence of a good and a better imply the existence of a best? This is playing with words. We invent the words and make arguments from them. The better is not a fact: it is only a word and a human judgement.'

'You are arguing,' I said, 'against someone who can't answer you back. You see, M. Morin, I don't believe either. I'm curious, that's all.'

'Ah,' he said, 'you've said that before – curious. Curiosity is a great trap. They used to come here in their dozens to see me. I used to get letters saying how I had converted them by this book or that. Long after I ceased to believe myself I was a carrier of belief, like a man can be a carrier of disease without being sick. Women especially.' He added with disgust, 'I had only to sleep with a woman to make a convert.' He turned his red eyes towards me and really seemed to require an answer when he said, 'What sort of Rasputin life was that?' The brandy by now had really taken a hold; I wondered how many years he had been waiting for some stranger without faith to whom he could speak with frankness.

'Did you never tell this to a priest? I always imagined in your faith . . .'

'There were always too many priests,' he said, 'around me. The priests swarmed like flies. Near me and any woman I knew. First I was an exhibit for their faith. I was useful to them, a sign that even an intelligent man could believe. That was the period of the Dominicans, who liked the literary atmosphere and good wine. Then afterwards when the books stopped, and they smelt something – gamey – in my religion, it was the turn of the Jesuits, who never despair of what they call a man's soul.'

'And why did the books stop?'

'Who knows? Did you never write verses for some girl when you were a boy?'

'Of course.'

'But you didn't marry the girl, did you? The unprofessional poet writes of his feelings and when the poem is finished he finds his love dead on the page. Perhaps I wrote away my belief like the young man writes away his love. Only it took longer – twenty years and fifteen books.' He held up the wine. 'Another glass?'

'I would rather have some of your brandy.' Unlike the wine it was a crude and common mark, and I thought again, For a beggar's sake or his own? I said, 'All the same you go to Mass.'

'I go to Midnight Mass on Christmas Eve,' he said. 'The worst of Catholics goes then – even those who do not go at Easter. It is the Mass of our childhood. And of mercy. What would they think if I were not there? I don't want to give scandal. You must realize I wouldn't speak to any one of my neighbours as I have spoken to you. I am their Catholic author, you see. Their Academician. I never wanted to help anyone to believe, but God knows I wouldn't take a hand in robbing them . . .'

'I was surprised at one thing when I saw you there, M. Morin.'

'Yes?'

76

I said rashly, 'You and I were the only ones who didn't take Communion.'

'That is why I don't go to the church in my own village. That too would be noticed and cause scandal.'

'Yes, I can see that.' I stumbled heavily on (perhaps the brandy had affected me too). 'Forgive me, M. Morin, but I wondered at your age what kept you from Communion. Of course now I know the reason.'

'Do you?' Morin said. 'Young man, I doubt it.' He looked at me across his glass with impersonal enmity. He said, 'You don't understand a thing I have been saying to you. What a story you would make of this if you were a journalist and yet there wouldn't be a word of truth . . .'

I said stiffly, 'I thought you made it perfectly clear that you had lost your faith.'

'Do you think that would keep anyone from the Confessional? You are a long way from understanding the Church or the human mind, Mr Dunlop. Why, it is one of the most common confessions of all for a priest to hear – almost as common as adultery. "Father, I have lost my faith." The priest, you may be sure, makes it himself often enough at the altar before he receives the Host.'

I said – I was angry in return now, 'Then what keeps you away? Pride? One of your Rasputin women?'

'As you so rightly thought,' he said, 'women are no longer a problem at my age.' He looked at his watch. 'Two-thirty. Perhaps I ought to drive you back.'

'No,' I said, 'I don't want to part from you like this. It's the drink that makes us irritable. Your books are still important to me. I know I am ignorant. I am not a Catholic and never shall be, but in the old days your books made me understand that at least it might be possible to believe. You never suddenly closed the door in my face as you are doing now. Nor did your characters, Durobier, Sagrin.' I indicated the brandy bottle. 'I told you just now – people are not only hungry and thirsty in that way. Because you've lost *your* faith . . .'

He interrupted me ferociously. 'I never told you that.'

'Then what have you been talking about all this time?'

'I told you I had lost my belief. That's quite a different thing. But how are you to understand?'

'You don't give me a chance.'

He was obviously striving to be patient. He said, 'I will put it this way. If a doctor prescribed you a drug and told you to take it every day for the rest of your life and you stopped obeying him and drank no more, and your health decayed, would you not have faith in your doctor all the more?'

'Perhaps. But I still don't understand you.'

'For twenty years,' Morin said, 'I excommunicated myself voluntarily. I never went to Confession. I loved a woman too much to pretend to myself that I would ever leave her. You know the condition of absolution? A firm purpose of amendment. I had no such purpose. Five years ago my mistress died and my sex died with her.'

'Then why couldn't you go back?'

'I was afraid. I am still afraid.'

'Of what the priest would say?'

'What a strange idea you have of the Church. No, not of what the priest would say. He would say nothing. I daresay there is no greater gift you can give a priest in the confessional, Mr Dunlop, than to return to it after many years. He feels of use again. But can't you understand? I can tell myself now that my lack of belief is a final proof that the Church is right and the faith is true. I had cut myself off for twenty years from grace and my belief withered as the priests said it would. I don't believe in God and His Son and His angels and His saints, but I know the reason why I don't believe and the reason is – the Church is true and what she taught me is true. For twenty years I have been without the sacraments and I can see the effect. The wafer must be more than wafer.'

'But if you went back ...'

'If I went back and belief did not return? That is what I fear, Mr Dunlop. As long as I keep away from the sacraments, my lack of belief is an argument for the Church. But if I returned and they failed me, then I would really be a man without faith, who had better hide himself quickly in the grave so as not to discourage others.' He laughed uneasily. 'Paradoxical, Mr Dunlop?'

'That is what they said of your books.'

'I know.'

'Your characters carried their ideas to extreme lengths. So your critics said.'

'And you think I do too?'

'Yes, M. Morin.'

His eyes wouldn't meet mine. He grimaced beyond me. 'At least I am not a carrier of disease any longer. You have escaped infection.' He added, 'Time for bed, Mr Dunlop. Time for bed. The young need more sleep.'

'I am not as young as that.'

'To me you seem very young.'

He drove me back to my hotel and we hardly spoke. I was thinking of the strange faith which held him even now after he had ceased to believe. I had felt very little curiosity since that moment of the war when I had spoken to the chaplain, but now I began to wonder again. M. Morin considered he had ceased to be a carrier, and I couldn't help hoping that he was right. He had forgotten to give me the address of the vineyard, but I had forgotten to ask him for it when I said good night.

DREAM OF A STRANGE LAND

1

THE house of the Herr Professor was screened on every side by the plantation of fir-trees which grew among great grey rocks. Although it was only twenty minutes' ride from the capital and then a few minutes from the main road to the north, a visitor had the impression that he was in deep country; he felt himself to be hundreds of miles away from the cafés, the kiosks, the opera-house and the theatres.

The Herr Professor had virtually retired two years ago when he reached the age of sixty-five. His appointment at the hospital had been filled, he had closed his consulting-room in the capital, and if he continued to work it was only for a few favoured patients who were compelled to drive out to see him, or if they were poor (for he had not clung to a few rich patients only) take a bus which landed them about ten minutes' walk away at the edge of the trees and the rocks.

It was one of these poorer patients who stood now in the doctor's study listening to his doom. The study had folding pitchpine doors leading to the living-room, which the patient had never seen. A heavy dark bookcase stood against the wall full of heavy dark books, all obviously medical in character (no one had ever seen the Herr Professor with any lighter literature, nor heard him give an opinion of even the most respected classic. Once questioned on Madame Bovary's poisoning, he had professed complete ignorance of the book, and another time he had shown himself to be equally ignorant of Ibsen's treatment of syphilis in *Ghosts*). The desk was as heavy and dark as the bookcase; it was only a desk as heavy which could have borne without cracking the massive bronze paperweight more than a foot high subrepresented Prometheus chained to his rock with a hovering eagle thrusting its beak into his liver. (Sometimes, when breaking the news to a patient with cirrhosis, the Professor had referred to his paperweight with dry humour.)

The patient wore a shabby-genteel suit of dark cloth; the

80

cuffs had frayed and been repaired. He wore stout boots which had seen just as long a service, and through the open door in the hall behind him hung an overcoat and an umbrella, while a pair of goloshes stood in the steel trough under the umbrella, the snow not yet melted from their uppers. He was a man past fifty who had spent all his adult years behind the counter of a bank and by patient labour and courtesy he had risen to the position of second cashier. He would never be first cashier, for the first cashier was at least five years younger.

The Herr Professor had a short grey beard and he wore old-fashioned glasses, steel-rimmed, for his short sight. His rather hairy hands were scattered with grave-marks. As he seldom smiled one had very little opportunity to see his strong and perfect teeth. He said firmly, caressing Prometheus as he spoke, 'I warned you when you first came that my treatment might have started too late – to arrest the disease. Now the smear-test shows . . .'

'But, Herr Professor, you have been treating me all these months. No one knows about it. I can go on working at the bank. Can't you continue to treat me a little longer?'

'I would be breaking the law,' the Herr Professor explained, making a motion as though his thumb and forefinger clutched a chalk. 'Contagious cases must always go to the hospital.'

'But you yourself, Professor, have said that it is one of the most difficult of all diseases to catch.'

'And yet you caught it.'

'How? How?' the patient asked himself with the weariness of a man who has confronted the same question time without mind.

'Perhaps it was when you were working on the coast. There are many contacts in a port.'

'Contacts?'

'I assume you are a man like other men.'

'But that was seven years ago.'

'One has known the disease to take ten years to develop.'

'It will be the end of my work, Herr Professor. The bank will never take me back. My pension will be very small.'

'You take an exaggerated view. After a certain period . . . Hansen's disease is quite curable.'

'Why don't you call it by its proper name?'

'The International Congress decided five years ago to change the name.'

'The world hasn't changed the name, Herr Professor. If you send me to that hospital, everyone will know that I am a leper.'

'I have no choice. But I assure you you will find it very comfortable. There is television, I believe, in every room, and a golf-course.'

The Herr Professor showed no impatience at all, unless the fact that he did not ask the patient to sit and stood himself, stiff and straight-backed behind Prometheus and the eagle, was a sign of it.

'Herr Professor, I implore you. I will not breathe a word to a soul. You can treat me just as well as the hospital can. You've said yourself that the risk of contagion is very small, Herr Professor. I have my savings – they are not very great, but I will give them all . . .'

'My dear sir, you must not try to bribe me. It is not only insulting, it is a gross error of taste. I am sorry. I must ask you to go now. My time is very much occupied.'

'Herr Professor, you have no idea what it means to me. I lead a very simple life, but if a man is alone in the world he grows to love his habits. I go to a café by the lake every day at seven o'clock and stay there till eight. They all know me in the café. Sometimes I play a game of checkers. On Sunday I take the lake steamer to –'

'Your habits will have to be interrupted for a year or two,' the Herr Professor said sharply.

'Interrupted? You say interrupted? But I can never go back. Never. Leprosy is a word – it isn't a disease. They'll never believe leprosy can be cured. You can't cure a word.'

'You will be getting a certificate signed by the hospital authorities,' the Herr Professor said.

'A certificate! I might just as well carry a bell.'

He moved to the door, the hall, his umbrella and the goloshes; the Herr Professor, with a sigh of relief which was almost inaudible beyond the room, seated himself at his desk.

But again the patient had turned back. 'Is it that you don't trust me to keep quiet, Herr Professor?'

'I have every belief, I can assure you, that you would keep quiet. For your own sake. But you cannot expect a doctor of my standing to break the law. A sensible and necessary law. If it had not been infringed somewhere by someone you would not be standing here today. Good-bye, Herr –', but the patient had already closed the outer door and had begun to walk back amongst the rocks and firs towards the road, the bus-stop and the capital. The Herr Professor went to the window to make sure that he was truly gone and saw him among the snow-flakes which drifted lightly between the trees; he paused once and gesticulated with his hands as though a new argument had occurred to him which he was practising on a rock. Then he padded on and disappeared from sight.

The Herr Professor opened the sliding doors of the dining-room and made his accurate way to the sideboard, which was heavy like his desk. Instead of the Prometheus there stood on it a large silver flagon inscribed with the Herr Professor's name and a date more than forty years past – an award for fencing – and beside it lay a large silver epergne, also inscribed, a present from the staff of the hospital on his retirement. The Herr Professor took a hard green apple and walked back to his study. He sat down at his desk again and his teeth went crunch, crunch, crunch.

2

Later that morning the Herr Professor received another caller, but this one arrived before the house in a Mercedes-Benz car and the Herr Professor went himself to the door to show him in.

'Herr Colonel,' he said as he pulled forward the only chair of any comfort to be found in his study, 'this I hope is only a friendly call and not a professional one.'

'I am never ill,' the Colonel said with a look of irritated amusement at the very idea. 'My blood-pressure is normal, my weight is what it should be, and my heart's sound. I function like a machine. Indeed I find it difficult to believe that this machine need ever wear out. I have no worries, my nervous system is perfectly adjusted . . .'

'Then I'm relieved to know, Herr Colonel, that this is a social call.'

'The army,' the Colonel went on, crossing his long slim legs encased in English tweed, 'is the most healthy profession possible – naturally I mean in a neutral country like ours. The annual manoeuvres do one a world of good, brace the system, clean the blood . . .'

'I wish I could recommend them to my patients.'

'Oh, we can't have sick men in the army.' The Colonel added with a dry laugh, 'We leave that to the warring nations. They can never have our efficiency.'

The Herr Professor offered the Colonel a cigar. The Colonel took a cutter from a little leather case and prepared the cigar. 'You have met the Herr General?' he asked.

'On one or two occasions.'

'He is celebrating his seventieth birthday tonight.'

'Really? A very well preserved man.'

'Naturally. Now his friends – of whom I count myself the chief – have been arranging a very special occasion for him. You know, of course, his favourite hobby?'

'I can't say . . .'

'The tables. For the last fifty years he has spent most of his leaves at Monte Carlo.'

'He too must have a good nervous system.'

'Of course. Now it occurred to his friends, since he cannot spend his birthday at Monte Carlo for reasons of a quite temporary indisposition, to bring, as it were, the tables to him.'

'How can that be possible?'

'Everything was satisfactorily arranged. A croupier from Cannes and two assistants. All the necessary equipment. One of my friends was to have lent us his house in the country. You understand that everything has to be very discreet because of our absurd laws. You would think the police on such an occasion would turn a blind eye, but among the higher officials there is a great jealousy of the army. I once heard the Commissioner remark – at a party to which I was surprised to see that he had been invited – that the only wars in which our country had ever been engaged were fought by *his* men.'

'I don't follow.'

'Oh, he was referring to crime. An absurd comparison. What has crime to do with war?'

The Herr Professor said, 'You were telling me that everything had been satisfactorily arranged . . .?'

'With the Herr General Director of the National Bank. But suddenly today he telephoned to say that a child – a girl as one might expect – had developed scarlatina. The household therefore is in quarantine.'

'The Herr General will be disappointed.'

'The Herr General knows nothing of all this. He understands that a party is being given in his honour in the country – that is all.'

'And you come to me,' the Herr Professor said, trying to hide mystification which he regarded as a professional weakness, 'in case I can suggest . . .?'

'I come to you, Herr Professor, quite simply to borrow your house for this evening. The problem can be reduced to very simple terms. The house has to be in the country – I have explained to you why. It must have a *salon* of a certain size – to receive the tables; we can hardly have less than three, since the guests will number about a hundred. And the owner of the house must naturally be acceptable to the Herr General. There are houses a great deal larger than yours that the General could not be expected to enter as a guest. We can hardly, in this case, requisition.'

'I am honoured, of course, Herr Colonel, but . . .'

'These doors slide back, I suppose, and can form a room sufficiently large . . .?'

'Yes, but . . .'

'Pardon me. You were saying?'

'I had the impression that the party was for tonight?'

'Yes.'

'I don't see how there could be time . . .'

'A matter of logistics, Herr Professor. Leave logistics to the army.' He took a notebook from his pocket and wrote down 'lights'. He explained to the Herr Professor, 'We shall have to hang chandeliers. A casino is unthinkable without chandeliers. May I see the other room, please?'

He paced it with his long tweed-clad legs. 'It will make a fine *salle privée* with the doors folded back and the chandeliers substituted for these – forgive me for saying so – rather commonplace centre lights. Your furniture we can store upstairs? Of course we will bring our own chairs. This sideboard, however, can serve as a bar. I see you were a fencer in your time, Herr Professor?'

'Yes.'

'The Herr General used to be very keen on fencing. Now tell me, where do you think we could put the orchestra?'

'Orchestra?'

'My regiment will supply the musicians. If the worst came to the worst I suppose they could play on the stairs.' He stood at the window of the *salon,* looking out at the wintry garden bounded by the dark wood of fir-trees. 'Is that a summerhouse?'

'Yes.'

'The oriental touch is very suitable. If they played there, and if we left a window a little open, the music will surely carry faintly . . .'

'The cold . . .'

'You have a fine stove and the curtains are heavy.'

'The summerhouse is altogether unheated.'

'The men can wear their military overcoats. And then for a fiddler, you know, the exercise . . .'

'And all this for tonight?'

'For tonight.'

The Herr Professor said, 'I have never before violated the law,' and then smiled a quick false smile to cover his failure of nerve.

'You could hardly do so in a better cause,' the Herr Colonel replied.

3

Long before dark the furniture-vans began to arrive. The chandeliers came first, with the wine-glasses, and remained crated in the hall until the electricians drove up, and then the

waiters arrived simultaneously with the van that contained
seventy-four small gilt chairs. The mover's men had beer in
the kitchen with the Herr Professor's housekeeper, waiting
for a lorry to turn up with the three roulette-tables. The
roulette-wheels, the cloths and the boxes of plastic tokens, of
varying colours and shapes according to value, were brought
later in a smart private car with the three croupiers, serious
men in black suits. The Herr Professor had never seen so many
cars parked before his house. He felt a stranger, a guest, and
lingered at his bedroom-window, afraid to go out on the stairs
and meet the workmen. The long passage outside his room
became littered with the furniture from below.

As the red winter sun sank in early afternoon below the
black firs the cars began to multiply upon the drive. First a
fleet of taxis arrived one behind the other, all bright yellow in
colour like an amber chain, and out of these scrambled many
burly men in military overcoats carrying musical instruments,
which too often stuck in the doors and had to be extricated
with care and difficulty: it was hard indeed to understand
how the 'cello had ever fitted in – the neck came out first like
a dressmaker's dummy and then the shoulders proved too
wide. The men in overcoats stood around holding violin-bows
like rifles at the ready, and a small man with a triangle shouted
advice. Presently they had all disappeared from the front of
the house and discordant sounds of tuning came across the
snow from the summerhouse built in oriental taste. Something broke in the passage outside, and the Herr Professor,
looking out, saw that it was one of the central lamps criticized
by the Herr Colonel, which had fallen off the occasional table
on which it had been propped. The passage was nearly
blocked by the heavy desk from the study, the glass-fronted
bookcase and his three filing cabinets. The Herr Professor
salvaged Prometheus and carried the bronze into his bedroom for safety, though it was the least fragile thing in all
the house. There was a sound of hammers below and the
Herr Colonel's voice could be heard giving orders. The Herr
Professor went back into his bedroom. He sat on the bed
and read a little Schopenhauer to soothe himself.

It was some three-quarters of an hour later that the Herr

Colonel found him there. He came briskly in, wearing regimental evening-dress, which made his legs thinner and longer than ever. 'Zero hour approaches,' he said, 'and we are all but ready. You would not recognize your house, Herr Professor. It is quite transformed. The Herr General will feel himself in a sunnier and more liberal clime. The musicians will play a pot-pourri of Strauss and Offenbach with a little of Lehar, which the Herr General finds more easy to recognize. I've seen to it that suitable paintings hang on the walls. You will realize when you come down and see the *salle privée* that this has been no ordinary military exercise. A care for detail marks a good soldier. Tonight, Herr Professor, your house has become a casino, by the Mediterranean. I had thought of masking the trees in some way, but there was no way of getting rid of the snow which continues to fall.'

'Astonishing,' the Herr Professor said. 'Quite astonishing.' From the distant summerhouse he could hear a melody from *La Belle Hélène,* and on the drive outside cars continually braked. He felt far from home as though he were living in a strange country.

'If you will excuse me,' he said, 'I will leave everything tonight in your hands. I hardly know the Herr General. I will have a sandwich quietly in my room.'

'Quite impossible,' the Herr Colonel said. 'You are the host. By this time the Herr General knows your name, although of course he hardly expects the sight which will greet ... Ah, the guests are now beginning to arrive. I asked them to come early so that by the time the Herr General puts in his appearance everything will be in full swing, the wheels turning, the stakes laid, the croupiers calling ... the field of battle stretched before him, *rouge et noir*. Come, Herr Professor, a little flutter at the tables – it is time for the two of us to open the ball.'

4

The road was treacherous under the thin and new-fallen snow; the bus from the capital proceeded at a pace no smarter than a practice-runner who is unwilling to strain a muscle before the great race. The patient's feet felt chilled even through his

goloshes, or perhaps it was the cold of his errand, a fool's
errand. There was a lot of traffic on the road that night:
yellow taxis frequently passed the bus, and small sports-cars
full of young men in uniform or evening-dress, laughing or
singing, and once at a particularly imperious siren – which
might have been that of a police-car or an ambulance – the
bus slithered awkwardly to a stop beside the blue heaps of
snow on the margin, and a big Benz went by; in it the patient
saw an old man sitting stiffly upright with a long grey moustache which might have dated from the neutrality of 1914,
wearing an old-fashioned uniform with a fur hat on his head,
pulled down over his ears.

The patient alighted at a halt beside the road; the moon
was nearly full, but he still required the pocket-torch which
he carried with him to show the way through the woods: no
headlights of cars helped him now on the private drive to
the Herr Professor's house. As he walked through the loose
snow at the edge of the road he tried to practise his final appeal. If that failed there was nothing for him but the hospital, unless he could summon enough courage to enter the icy
water of the lake and never to return. He felt very little hope,
and, for some reason that he could not understand, when he
tried to visualize the Herr Professor at his desk – angry and
impatient at this so late and unforeseen a visit – he could see
only the half-spread wings of the bronze eagle and the jutting
beak fastened in the intestines of the prisoner.

He pleaded in an undertone beneath the trees, 'There would
be no danger to anyone at all, Herr Professor. I have always
been a lonely man. I have no parents. My only sister died
last year. I see no one, speak to no one except the clients in
the bank. An occasional game of checkers in the café perhaps
– that is all. I would cut myself off even further, Herr Professor
if you thought it wiser. As for the bank, I have always been in
the habit of wearing gloves when I handle the notes – so many
are filthy. I will take any precaution you suggest if you will
go on treating me in private, Herr Professor. I am a law-
abiding man, but surely the spirit is more important than the
letter. I will abide by the spirit.'

The eagle gripped Prometheus with its unrelenting beak,

and the patient said sadly as though to prevent the repetition of a phrase he could not bear to hear again, 'I don't like television, Herr Professor – it makes my eyes water, and I have never played golf.'

He halted under the trees, and a lump of snow from a burdened branch fell with a plomp upon his umbrella. It seemed very unlikely, but he thought that he heard strains of distant music borne on a gust of wind and borne away again. He even thought he recognized the melody, something from *La Vie Parisienne,* a waltz sounding for a moment from where the darkness and the snow lay all around. He had seen this place before only in daylight; the snow touched his face, and the stars crackled overhead between the firs; he felt as though he must have missed his path and entered a strange estate where perhaps a dance was in progress . . .

But when he reached the circular drive before the house he recognized the portico, the shape of the windows, the steep slope of the roof from which at intervals the snow slid with a crunch like a man eating apples. It was all that he could recognize, for he had never seen the house like this, ablaze with light and noisy with voices. Perhaps two neighbouring estates had been built by the same architect, and somehow in the wood he had taken the wrong turning. To make sure, he approached the windows, the hard snow breaking like biscuits under his goloshes.

Two young officers, who were obviously the worse for drink, staggered out from the open doorway. 'I have been betrayed by nineteen,' one of them said, 'that confounded nineteen.'

'And I by zero. I have been faithful to zero for an hour, but not once . . .'

The first young man took a revolver from the holster at his side and waved it in the moonlight. 'All that is required now,' he said, 'is a suicide. The atmosphere is imperfect without one.'

'Be careful. It might be loaded.'

'It *is* loaded. Who is that man?'

'I don't know. The gardener probably. Don't fool about with that thing.'

'More bubbly is required,' the first man said. He tried to put his revolver back into the holster, but it slid down into the snow and he carefully secured the empty holster. 'More bubbly,' he repeated, 'before the dream fades.' They moved erratically back into the house. The dark object made a pocket in the snow.

The patient went up to the window, which should, if he had taken the right path, have been the window of the Herr Professor's study, but now he realized for certain that in the darkness he had come to the wrong house. Instead of a small square room with heavy desk and heavy bookcase and steel filing-cabinets was a long room brilliantly lit with cut-glass chandeliers, the walls hung with pictures of dubious taste – young women in diaphanous nightgowns leaning over waterfalls or paddling among water-lilies in a stooping position. A crowd of men wearing uniform and evening-dress swarmed around three roulette tables, and the croupiers' cries came thinly out into the night, '*Faites vos jeux, messieurs, faites vos jeux,*' while somewhere in the black garden an orchestra was playing 'The Blue Danube'. The patient stood motionless in the snow, with his face pressed to the glass, and he thought, The wrong house? But this is not the wrong house; it is the wrong country. He felt that he could never find his way home from here – it was too far away.

At one of the tables, on the right of the croupier, sat the old man whom he had seen pass in the Mercedes-Benz. One hand was playing with his moustache, the other with a pile of tokens before him, counting and rearranging them while the ball span and jumped and span, and one foot beat in time to the tune from *The Merry Widow*. A champagne cork from the bar shot diagonally up and struck the chandelier while the croupiers cried again, '*Faites vos jeux. Faites vos jeux, messieurs,*' and the stem of a glass went crack in somebody's fingers.

Then the patient saw the Herr Professor standing with his back to the window at the other end of the great room, beyond the second chandelier, and they regarded each other, with the laughter and cries and glitter of light between them.

The Herr Professor could not properly see the patient – only the outline of a face pressed to the exterior of the pane,

91

but the patient could see the Herr Professor very clearly between the tables, in the light of the chandelier. He could even see his expression, the lost look on his face like that of someone who has come to the wrong party. The patient raised his hand, as though to indicate to the other that he was lost too, but of course the Herr Professor could not see the gesture in the dark. The patient realized quite clearly that, though they had once been well known to each other, it was quite impossible for them to meet, in this house to which they had both strayed by some strange accident. There was no consulting-room here, no file on his case, no desk, no Prometheus, no doctor even to whom he could appeal. *'Faites vos jeux, messieurs'* the croupiers cried, *'faites vos jeux.'*

5

The Herr Colonel said, 'My dear Herr Professor, after all, you are the host. You should at least lay one stake upon the table.' He took the Herr Professor by his sleeve and led him to the board where the Herr General sat, beating tip, tap, tip to the music of Lehar.

'The Herr Professor wishes to follow your fortune, Herr General.'

'I have little luck tonight, but let him . . .' and the General's fingers wove a design over the cloth. 'At the same time guard yourself with the zero.'

The ball span and jumped and span and came to rest. 'Zero,' the croupier announced and began to rake the other stakes in.

'At least you have not lost, Herr Professor,' the Herr General said. Somewhere far away behind the voices there was a faint explosion.

'The corks are popping,' the Herr Colonel said. 'Another glass of champagne, Herr General?'

'I had hoped it was a shot,' the Herr General said with a rather freezing smile. 'Ah, the old days . . . I remember once in Monte . . .'

The Herr Professor looked at the window, where he had thought a moment ago that someone looked in as lost as himself, but no one was there.

A DISCOVERY IN THE WOODS

1

THE village lay among the great red rocks about a thousand feet up and five miles from the sea, which was reached by a path that wound along the contours of the hills. No one in Pete's village had ever travelled further, though Pete's father had once, while fishing, encountered men from another small village beyond the headland, which stabbed the sea twenty miles to the east. The children, when they didn't accompany their fathers to the shingled cove in which the boats lay, would climb up higher for their games – of 'Old Noh' and 'Ware that Cloud' – below the red rocks that dominated their home. Low scrub a few hundred feet up gave place to woodland: trees clung to the rock-face like climbers caught in an impossible situation, and among the trees were the bushes of blackberry, the biggest fruits always sheltered from the sun. In the right season the berries formed a tasty sharp dessert to the invariable diet of fish. It was, taking it all in all, a sparse and simple yet a happy life.

Pete's mother was a little under five feet tall; she had a squint and she was inclined to stumble when she walked, but her movements to Pete seemed at their most uncertain the height of human grace, and when she told him stories, as she often did on the fifth day of the week, her stammer had for him the magical effect of music. There was one word in particular 't-t-t-tree' which fascinated him. 'What is it?' he would ask, and she would try to explain. 'You mean an oak?' 'A t-tree is not an oak. But an oak is a t-t-tree, and so is a b-birch.' 'But a birch is quite different from an oak. Anyone can tell they are not the same, even a long way off, like a dog and a cat.' 'A dog and a c-cat are both animals.' She had from some past generation inherited this ability to generalize, of which he and his father were quite incapable.

Not that he was a stupid child unable to learn from experience. He could even with some difficulty look back into the past for four winters, but the furthest time he could remember was very like a sea-fog, which the wind may disperse for a moment from a rock or a group of trees, but it closes down again. His mother claimed that he was seven years old, but his father said that he was nine and that after one more winter he would be old enough to join the crew of the boat which his father shared with a relation (everybody in the village was in some way related). Perhaps his mother had deliberately distorted his age to postpone the time when he would have to go fishing with the men. It was not only the question of danger – though every winter brought a mortal casualty along with it, so that the size of the village hardly increased more than a colony of ants; it was also the fact that he was the only child. (There were two sets of parents in the village, the Torts and the Foxes, who had more than one child, and the Torts had triplets.) When the time came for Pete to join his father, his mother would have to depend on other people's children for blackberries in the autumn, or just go without, and there was nothing she loved better than blackberries with a splash of goat's milk.

So this, he believed, was to be the last autumn on land, and he was not much concerned about it. Perhaps his father was in the right about his age, for he had become aware that his position as leader of a special gang was now too incontestable: his muscles felt the need of strengthening against an opponent greater than himself. His gang consisted this October of four children, to three of whom he had allotted numbers, for this made his commands sound more abrupt and discipline so much the easier. The fourth member was a seven-year-old girl called Liz, unwillingly introduced for reasons of utility.

They met among the ruins at the edge of the village. The ruins had always been there, and at night the children, if not the adults too, believed them to be haunted by giants. Pete's mother, who was far superior in knowledge to all the other women in the village, nobody knew why, said that her grandmother had spoken of a great catastrophe which thousands of years ago had involved a man called Noh – perhaps it was a thunderbolt from the sky, a huge wave (it would have needed a wave at least a thousand feet high to have extinguished this village), or maybe a plague, so some of the legends went, that had killed the inhabitants and left these ruins to the slow destruction of time. Whether the giants were the phantoms of the slayers or of the slain the children were never quite clear.

The blackberries this particular autumn were nearly over and in any case the bushes that grew within a mile of the village – which was called Bottom, perhaps because it lay at the foot of the red rocks – had been stripped bone-bare. When the gang had gathered at the rendezvous Pete made a revolutionary proposal – that they should enter a new territory in search of fruit.

Number One said disapprovingly, 'We've never done that before.' He was in all ways a conservative child. He had small deep-sunk eyes like holes in stone made by the dropping of water, and there was practically no hair on his head and that gave him the air of a shrivelled old man.

'We'll get into trouble,' Liz said, 'if we do.'

'Nobody need know,' Pete said, 'so long as we take the oath.'

The village by long custom claimed that the land belonging to it extended in a semi-circle three miles deep from the last cottage – even though the last cottage was a ruin of which only the foundations remained. Of the sea too they reckoned to own the water for a larger, more ill-defined area that extended some twelve miles out to sea. This claim, on the occasion when they encountered the boats from beyond the headland, nearly caused a conflict. It was Pete's father who made peace by pointing towards the clouds which had begun to mass over the horizon, one cloud in particular of enormous black menace, so that both parties turned in agreement towards the land, and the fishermen from the village beyond the headland never sailed again so far from their home. (Fishing was always done in grey overcast weather or in fine blue clear weather, or even during moonless nights, when the stars were sufficiently obscured; it was only when the shape of the clouds could be discerned that by general consent fishing stopped.)

'But suppose we meet someone?' Number Two asked.

'How could we?' Pete said.

A SENSE OF REALITY

'There must be a reason,' Liz said, 'why they don't want us to go.'

'There's no reason,' Pete said, 'except the law.'

'Oh, if it's only the law,' Number Three said, and he kicked a stone to show how little he thought of the law.

'Who does the land belong to?' Liz asked.

'To nobody,' Pete said. 'There's no one there at all.'

'All the same nobody has rights,' Number One said sententiously, looking inwards, with his watery sunk eyes.

'You are right there,' Pete said. 'Nobody has.'

'But I didn't mean what you mean,' Number One replied.

'You think there are blackberries there, further up?' Number Two asked. He was a reasonable child who only wanted to be assured that a risk was worth while.

'There are bushes all the way up through the woods,' Pete said.

'How do you know?'

'It stands to reason.'

It seemed odd to him that day how reluctant they were to take his advice. Why should the blackberry-bushes abruptly stop their growth on the border of their own territory? Blackberries were not created for the special use of Bottom. Pete said, 'Don't you want to pick them one time more before the winter comes?' and they hung their heads, as though they were seeking a reply in the red earth where the ants made roads from stone to stone. At last Number One said, 'Nobody's been there before,' as if that was the worst thing he could think of to say.

'All the better blackberries,' Pete replied.

Number Two said after consideration, 'The wood looks deeper up there and blackberries like the shade.'

Number Three yawned. 'Who cares about blackberries anyway? There's other things to do than pick. It's new ground, isn't it? Let's go and see. Who knows . . .?'

'Who knows?' Liz repeated in a frightened way and looked first at Pete and then at Number Three as though it were possible that perhaps *they* might.

'Hold up your hands and vote,' Pete said. He shot his own arm commandingly up and Number Three was only a second

96

behind. After a little hesitation Number Two followed suit; then, seeing that there was a majority anyway for going further, Liz raised a cautious hand but with a backward glance at Number One. 'So you're for home?' Pete said to Number One with scorn and relief.

'He'll have to take the oath anyway,' Number Three said, 'or else . . .'

'I don't have to take the oath if I'm going home.'

'Of course you have to or else you'll tell.'

'What do I care about your silly oath? It doesn't mean a thing. I can take it and tell just the same.'

There was a silence: the other three looked at Pete. The whole foundation of their mutual trust seemed to be endangered. No one had ever suggested breaking the oath before. At last Number Three said, 'Let's bash him.'

'No,' Pete said. Violence, he knew, was not the answer. Number One would run home just the same and tell everything. The whole blackberry-picking would be spoilt by the thought of the punishment to come.

'Oh hell,' Number Two said. 'Let's forget the blackberries and play Old Noh.'

Liz, like the girl she was, began to weep. 'I want to pick blackberries.'

But Pete had been given time to reach his decision. He said, 'He's going to take the oath and he's going to pick blackberries too. Tie his hands.'

Number One tried to escape, but Number Two tripped him up. Liz bound his wrists with her hair-ribbon, pulling a hard knot which only she knew – it was for such special skills as this that she had gained her entry into the gang. Number One sat on a chunk of ruin and sneered at them. 'How do I pick blackberries with my hands tied?'

'You were greedy and ate them all. You brought none home. They'll find the stains all over your clothes.'

'Oh, he'll get such a beating,' Liz said with admiration. 'I bet they'll beat him bare.'

'Four against one.'

'Now you are going to take the oath,' Pete said. He broke off two twigs and held them in the shape of a cross. Each of the other three members of the gang gathered saliva in the mouth and smeared the four ends of the cross. Then Pete thrust the sticky points of wood between the lips of Number One. Words were unnecessary: the same thought came inevitably to the mind of everyone with the act: 'Strike me dead if I tell.' After they had dealt forcibly with Number One each followed the same ritual. (Not one of them knew the origin of the oath; it had passed down through generations of such gangs. Once Pete, and perhaps all the others at one time or another had done the same in the darkness of bed, tried to explain to himself the ceremony of the oath: in sharing the spittle maybe they were sharing each other's lives, like mixing blood, and the act was solemnized upon a cross because for some reason a cross always signified shameful death.)

'Who's got a bit of string?' Pete said.

They tied the string to Liz's hair-ribbon and jerked Number One to his feet. Number Two pulled the string and Number Three pushed from behind. Pete led the way, upwards and into the wood, while Liz trailed alone behind; she couldn't move quickly because she had very bandy legs. Now that he realized there was nothing to be done about it, Number One made little trouble; he contented himself with an occasional sneer and lagged enough to keep the cord stretched tight, so that their march was delayed, and nearly two hours passed before they came to the edge of the known territory, emerging from the woods of Bottom on to the edge of a shallow ravine. On the other side the rocks rose again in exactly the same way, with the birch-trees lodged in every crevice up to the sky-line, to which no one from the village of Bottom had ever climbed; in all the interstices of roots and rocks the blackberries grew. From where they stood they could imagine they saw a blue haze like autumn smoke from the great luscious untouched fruit dangling in the shade.

2

All the same they hesitated a while before they started going down; it was as though Number One retained a certain malevolent influence and they had bound themselves to it by the cord. He squatted on the ground and sneered up at them. 'You see you don't dare . . .'

'Dare what?' Pete asked, trying to brush his words away before any doubts could settle on Two or Three or Liz and sap the uncertain power he still possessed.

'Those blackberries don't belong to us,' One said.

'Then who do they belong to?' Pete asked him, noting how Number Two looked at Number One as though he expected an answer.

Three said with scorn, 'Finding's keeping,' and kicked a stone down into the ravine.

'They belong to the next village. You know that as well as I do.'

'And where's the next village?' Pete asked.

'Somewhere.'

'For all you know there isn't another village.'

'There must be. It's common sense. We can't be the only ones – we and Two Rivers.' That was what they called the village which lay beyond the headland.

'But how do you *know*?' Pete said. His thoughts took wing. 'Perhaps we *are* the only ones. Perhaps we could climb up there and go on for ever and ever. Perhaps the world's empty.' He could feel that Number Two and Liz were half-way with him – as for Number Three he was a hopeless case; he cared for nothing. But all the same, if he had to choose his successor, he would prefer Number Three's care-for-nothing character than the elderly inherited rules of Number One or the unadventurous reliability of Number Two.

Number One said, 'You are just crazy,' and spat down into the ravine. 'We couldn't be the only ones alive. It's common sense.'

'Why not?' Pete said. 'Who knows?'

'Perhaps the blackberries are poisoned,' Liz said. 'Perhaps we'll get the gripes. Perhaps there's savages there. Perhaps there's giants.'

'I'll believe in giants when I see them,' Pete said. He knew how shallow her fear was; she only wanted to be reassured by someone stronger.

99

'You talk a lot,' Number One said, 'but you can't even organize. Why didn't you tell us to bring baskets if we were going to pick things?'

'We don't need baskets. We've got Liz's skirt.'

'And it's Liz who'll be thrashed when her skirt's all stained.'

'Not if it's full of blackberries she won't. Tie up your skirt, Liz.'

Liz tied it up, making it into a pannier in front, with a knot behind just above the opening of her small plump buttocks. The boys watched her with interest to see how she fixed it. 'They'll all fall out,' Number One said. 'You ought to have taken the whole thing off an' made a sack.'

'How could I climb holding a sack? You don't know a thing, Number One. I can fix this easy.' She squatted on the ground with a bare buttock on each heel and tied and retied the knot till she was quite satisfied that it was firm.

'So now we go down,' Number Three said.

'Not till I give the order. Number One, I'll release you if you promise to give no trouble.'

'I'll give plenty of trouble.'

'Number Two and Three, you take charge of Number One. You're the rear-guard, see. If we have to retreat in a hurry, you just leave the prisoner behind. Liz and I go ahead to reconnoitre.'

'Why Liz?' Number Three said. 'What good's a girl?'

'In case we have to use a spy. Girl spies are always best. Anyway they wouldn't bash a girl.'

'Pa does,' Liz said, twitching her buttocks.

'But I want to be in the van,' Three said.

'We don't know which is the van yet. They may be watching us now while we talk. They may be luring us on, and then they'll attack in the rear.'

'You're afraid,' Number One said. 'Fainty goose! Fainty goose!'

'I'm not afraid, but I'm boss, I'm responsible for the gang. Listen all of you, in case of danger we give one short whistle. Stay where you are. Don't move. Don't breathe. Two short whistles mean abandon the prisoner and retreat double-quick.

One long whistle means treasure discovered, all well, come as quick as you can. Everybody got that clear?'

'Yah,' said Number Two. 'But suppose we're just lost?'

'Stay where you are and wait for a whistle.'

'Suppose *he* whistles – to confuse?' Number Two asked, digging at Number One with his toe.

'If he does gag him. Gag him hard, so his teeth squeak.'

Pete went to the edge of the plateau and gazed down, to choose his path through the scrub; the rocks descended some thirty feet. Liz stood close behind him and held the edge of his shirt. 'Who are *They*?' she whispered.

'Strangers.'

'You don't believe in giants?'

'No.'

'When I think of giants, I shiver – here,' 'and she laid her hand on the little bare mount of Venus below her panniered skirt.

Pete said, 'We'll start down there between those clumps of gorse. Be careful. The stones are loose and we don't want to make any noise at all.' He turned back to the others, who watched him with admiration, envy and hate (that was Number One). 'Wait till you see us start climbing up the other side and then you come on down.' He looked at the sky. 'The invasion began at noon,' he announced with the precision of an historian recording an event in the past which had altered the shape of the world.

3

'We could whistle now,' Liz suggested. They were half-way up the slope of the ravine by this time, out of breath from the scramble. She put a blackberry in her mouth and added, 'They're sweet. Sweeter than ours. Shall I start picking?' Her thighs and bottom were scratched with briars and smeared with blood the colour of blackberry juice.

Pete said, 'Why, I've seen better than these in our territory. Liz, don't you notice, not one of them's been picked. No one's ever come here. These ones are nothing to what we'll find later. They've been growing for years and years and years – why, I wouldn't be surprised if we came on a whole forest of them with bushes as high as trees and berries as big as apples. We'll leave the little ones for the others if they want to pick them. You and I will climb up higher and find real treasure.' As he spoke he could hear the scrape of the others' shoes and the roll of a loose stone, but they could see nothing because the bushes grew so thick around the trees. 'Come on. If we find treasure first, it's ours.'

'I wish it was real treasure, not just blackberries.'

'It might be real treasure. No one's ever explored here before us.'

'Giants?' Liz asked him with a shiver.

'Those are stories they tell children. Like Old Noh and his ship. There never were giants.'

'Not Noh?'

'What a baby you are.'

They climbed up and up among the birches and bushes, and the sound of the others diminished below them. There was a different smell here: hot and moist and metallic, far away from the salt of the sea. Then the trees and bushes thinned and they were at the summit of the hills. When they looked backwards, Bottom was hidden by the ridge between, but through the trees they could see a line of blue as though the sea had been lifted up almost to their level by some gigantic convulsion. They turned nervously away from it and stared into the unknown land ahead.

4

'It's a house,' Liz said. 'It's a huge house.'

'It can't be. You've never seen a house that size – or that shape,' but he knew that Liz was right. This had been made by men and not by nature. It was something in which people had once lived.

'A house for giants,' Liz said fearfully.

Pete lay on his stomach and peered over the edge of the ravine. A hundred feet down among the red rocks lay a long structure glinting here and there among the bushes and moss which overgrew it – it stretched beyond their sight, trees climbed along its sides, trees had seeded on the roof, and up the length of two enormous chimneys ivy twined and flowering plants with trumpet-mouths. There was no smoke, no sign of any occupant; only the birds, perhaps disturbed by their voices, called warnings among the trees, and a colony of starlings rose from one of the chimneys and dispersed.

'Let's go back,' Liz whispered.

'We can't now,' Pete said. 'Don't be afraid. It's only another ruin. What's wrong with ruins? We've always played in them.'

'It's scary. It's not like the ruins at Bottom.'

'Bottom's not the world,' Pete said. It was the expression of a profound belief he shared with no one else.

The huge structure was tilted at an angle, so that they could almost see down one of the enormous chimneys, which gaped like a hole in the world. 'I'm going down to look,' Pete said, 'but I'll spy out the land first.'

'Shall I whistle?'

'Not yet. Stay where you are in case the others come.'

He moved with caution along the ridge. Behind him the strange thing – not built of stone or wood – extended a hundred yards or more, sometimes hidden, sometimes obscured by trees, but in the direction he now took the cliff was bare of vegetation, and he was able to peer down at the great wall of the house, not straight but oddly curved, like the belly of a fish or . . . He stood still for a moment, looking hard at it: the curve was the enormous magnification of something that was familiar to him. He went thoughtfully on, pondering on the old legend which had been the subject of their games. Nearly a hundred yards further he stopped again. It was as though at this point some enormous hand had taken the house and split it in two. He could look down between the two portions and see the house exposed floor by floor – there must be five, six, seven of them, with nothing stirring inside, except where the bushes had found a lodging and a wing flickered. He could imagine the great halls receding into the dark, and he thought how all the inhabitants of Bottom could have lived in a single room on a single floor and still have found space for their animals and their gear. How many thousand people, he wondered, had once lived in this enormous house? He hadn't realized the world contained so many.

103

When the house was broken – how? – one portion had been flung upwards at an angle, and only fifty yards from where he stood he could see where the end of it penetrated the ridge, so that if he wished to explore further he had only to drop a few yards to find himself upon the roof. There trees grew again and made an easy descent. He had no excuse to stay, and suddenly aware of loneliness and ignorance and the mystery of the great house he put his fingers to his mouth and gave one long whistle to summon all the others.

5

They were overawed too, and if Number One had not so jeered at them, perhaps they would have decided to go home with the secret of the house locked in their minds with a dream of one day returning. But when Number One said, 'Softies, Fainties . . .' and shot his spittle down towards the house, Number Three broke silence. 'What are we waiting for?' Then Pete had to act, if he was to guard his leadership. Scrambling from branch to branch of a tree that grew from a plateau of rock below the ridge, he got within six feet of the roof and dropped. He landed on his knees upon a surface cold and smooth as an egg-shell. The four children looked down at him and waited.

The slope of the roof was such that he had to slide cautiously downwards on his bottom. At the end of the descent there was another house which had been built upon the roof, and he realized from where he sat that the whole structure was not one house but a succession of houses built one over the other, and above the topmost house loomed the tip of the enormous chimney. Remembering how the whole thing had been torn apart, he was careful not to slide too fast for fear that he should plunge into the gap between. None of the others had followed him; he was alone.

Ahead of him was a great arch of some unknown material, and below the arch a red rock rose and split it in two. This was like a victory for the mountains; however hard the material men had used in making the house, the mountains remained the stronger. He came to rest with his feet against a rock and looked down into the wide gap where the rock had come up and split the houses; the gap was many yards across; it was bridged by a fallen tree, and although he could see but a little way down, he had the same sense which he had received above that he was looking into something as deep as the sea. Why was it he half expected to see fishes moving there?

With his hand pressed on the needle of red rock he stood upright and, looking up, was startled to see two unwinking eyes regarding him from a few feet away. Then as he moved again he saw that they belonged to a squirrel, the colour of the rock: it turned without hurry or fear, lifted a plumy tail and neatly evacuated before it leapt into the hall ahead of him.

The hall – it was indeed a hall, he realized, making his way towards it astride the fallen tree, and yet the first impression he had was of a forest, with the trees regularly spaced as in a plantation made by men. It was possible to walk there on a level, though the ground was hummocked with red rock which here and there had burst through the hard paving. The trees were not trees at all but pillars of wood, which still showed in patches a smooth surface, but pitted for most of their length with worm-holes and draped with ivy that climbed to the roof fifty feet up to escape through a great tear in the ceiling. There was a smell of vegetation and damp, and all down the hall were dozens of small green tumuli like woodland-graves.

He kicked one of the mounds with a foot and it disintegrated immediately below the thick damp moss that covered it. Gingerly he thrust his hand into the soggy greenery and pulled out a strut of rotting wood. He moved on and tried again a long curved hump of green which stood more than breast-high – not like a common grave – and this time he stubbed his toes and winced with the pain. The greenery had taken no root here, but had spread from tumulus to hump across the floor, and he was able to pluck away without difficulty the leaves and tendrils. Underneath lay a stone slab in many beautiful colours, green and rose-pink and red the colour of blood. He moved around it, cleaning the surface as he went, and here at last he came on real treasure. For a moment he did not realize what purpose those half-translucent objects could have served; they stood in rows behind a smashed panel, most broken into green rubble, but a few intact, except for the discoloration of age. It was from their shape he realized that they must once have been drinking pots, made of a material quite different from the rough clay to which he was accustomed. Scattered on the floor below were hundreds of hard round objects stamped with the image of a human head like those his grandparents had dug up in the ruins of Bottom – objects useless except that with their help it was possible to draw a perfect circle and they could be used as forfeits, in place of pebbles, in the game of 'Ware that Cloud'. They were more interesting than pebbles. They had dignity and rareness which belonged to all old things made by man – there was so little to be seen in the world older than an old man. He was tempted momentarily to keep the discovery to himself, but what purpose would they serve if they were not employed? A forfeit was of no value kept secret in a hole, so, putting his fingers to his mouth, he blew the long whistle again.

While waiting for the others to join him, he sat on the stone-slab deep in thought and pondered all he had seen, especially that great wall like a fish's belly. The whole huge house, it seemed to him, was like a monstrous fish thrown up among the rocks to die, but what a fish and what a wave to carry it so high.

The children came sliding down the roof, Number One still in tow between them; they gave little cries of excitement and delight; they were quite forgetful of their fear, as though it were the season of snow. Then they picked themselves up by the red rock, as he had done, straddled the fallen tree, and hobbled across the vast space of the hall, like insects caught under a cup.

'There's treasure for you,' Pete said with pride and he was glad to see them surprised into silence at the spectacle; even Number One forgot to sneer, and the cord by which they held him trailed neglected on the ground. At last Number Two said, 'Coo! It's better than blackberries.'

'Put the forfeits into Liz's skirt. We'll divide them later.'

'Does Number One get any?' Liz asked.

'There's enough for all,' Pete said. 'Let him go.' It seemed the moment for generosity, and in any case they needed all their hands. While they were gathering up the forfeits he went to one of the great gaps in the wall that must once have been windows, covered perhaps like the windows of Bottom with straw mats at night, and leant far out. The hills rose and fell, a brown and choppy sea; there was no sign of a village anywhere, not even of a ruin. Below him the great black wall curved out of sight; the place where it touched the ground was hidden by the tops of trees that grew in the valley below. He remembered the old legend, and the game they played among the ruins of Bottom. 'Noh built a boat. What kind of a boat? A boat for all the beasts and Brigit too. What kind of beasts? Big beasts like bears and beavers and Brigit too . . .'

Something went twang with a high musical sound and then there was a sigh which faded into silence. He turned and saw that Number Three was busy at yet another mound – the second biggest mound in the hall. He had unearthed a long box full of the oblongs they called dominoes, but every time he touched a piece a sound came, each a little different, and when he touched one a second time it remained silent. Number Two, in the hope of further treasure, groped in the mound and found only rusty wires which scratched his hands. No more sounds were to be coaxed out of the box, and no one ever discovered why at the beginning it seemed to sing to them.

6

Had they ever experienced a longer day even at the height of mid-summer? The sun, of course, stayed longer on the high plateau, and they could not tell how far night was already encroaching on the woods and valleys below them. There were two long narrow passages in the house down which they raced, tripping sometimes on the broken floor – Liz kept to the rear, unable to run fast for fear of spilling the forfeits from her skirt. The passages were lined with rooms, each one large enough to contain a family from Bottom, with strange tarnished twisted fixtures of which the purpose remained a mystery. There was another great hall, this one without pillars, which had a great square sunk in the floor lined with coloured stone; it shelved upwards, so that at one end it was ten feet deep and at the other so shallow that they could drop down to the drift of dead leaves and the scraps of twigs blown there by winter winds, and everywhere the droppings of birds like splashes of soiled snow.

At the end of yet a third hall they came, all of them, to a halt, for there in front of them, in bits and pieces, were five children staring back, a half-face, a head cut in two as though by a butcher's hatchet, a knee severed from a foot. They stared at the strangers and one of them defiantly raised a fist – it was Number Three. At once one of the strange flat children lifted his fist in reply. Battle was about to be joined; it was a relief in this empty world to find real enemies to fight, so they advanced slowly like suspicious cats, Liz a little in the rear, and there on the other side was another girl with skirts drawn up in the same fashion as hers to hold the same forfeits, with a similar little crack under the mount below the belly, but her face obscured with a green rash, one eye missing. The strangers moved their legs and arms, and yet remained flat against the wall, and suddenly they were touching nose to nose, and there was nothing there at all but the cold smooth wall. They backed away and approached and backed away: this was something not one of them could understand. So without saying anything to each other, in a private awe, they moved away to where steps led down to the floors below; there they hesitated again, listening and peering, their voices twittering against the unbroken silence, but they were afraid of the darkness, where the side of the mountain cut off all light, so they ran away and screamed defiantly down the long passages, where the late sun slanted in, until they came to rest at last in a group on the great stairs which led upwards into brighter daylight where the enormous chimneys stood.

'Let's go home,' Number One said. 'If we don't go, soon it will be dark.'

'Who's a Faintie now?' Number Three said.

'It's only a house. It's a big house, but it's only a house.'

Pete said, 'It's not a house,' and they all turned and looked their questions at him.

'What do you mean, not a house?' Number Two asked.

108

'It's a boat,' Pete said.

'You are crazy. Whoever saw a boat as big as this?'

'Whoever saw a house as big as this?' Liz asked.

'What's a boat doing on top of a mountain? Why would a boat have chimneys? What would a boat have forfeits for? When did a boat have rooms and passages?' They threw their sharp objections at him, like handfuls of gravel to sting him into sense.

'It's Noh's boat,' Pete said.

'You're nuts,' Number One said. 'Noh's a game. There was never anyone called Noh.'

'How can we tell? Maybe he did live hundreds of years ago. And if he had all the beasts with him, what could he do without lots of cages? Perhaps those aren't rooms along the passage there; perhaps they are cages.'

'And that hole in the floor?' Liz asked. 'What's that for?'

'I've been thinking about it. It might be a tank for water. Don't you see, he'd have to have somewhere to keep the water-rats and the tadpoles.'

'I don't believe it,' Number One said. 'How would a boat get up here?'

'How would a house as big as this get up here? You know the story. It floated here, and then the waters went down again and left it.'

'Then Bottom was at the bottom of the sea once?' Liz asked. Her mouth fell open and she scratched her buttocks stung with briars and scraped with rock and smeared with bird-droppings.

'Bottom didn't exist then. It was all so long ago . . .'

'He might be right,' Number Two said. Number Three made no comment: he began to mount the stairs towards the roof, and Pete followed quickly and overtook him. The sun lay flat across the tops of the hills which looked like waves, and in all the world there seemed to be nobody but themselves. The great chimney high above shot out a shadow like a wide black road. They stood silent, awed by its size and power, where it tilted towards the cliff above them. Then Number Three said, 'Do you really believe it?'

'I think so.'

'What about all our other games? "Ware that Cloud".'

'It may have been the cloud which frightened Noh.'

'But where did everybody go? There aren't any corpses.'

'There wouldn't be. Remember the game. When the water went down, they all climbed off the boat two by two.'

'Except the water-rats. The water went down too quickly and one of them was stranded. We ought to find *his* corpse.'

'It was hundreds of years ago. The ants would have eaten him.'

'Not the bones, they couldn't eat those.'

'I'll tell you something I saw – in those cages. I didn't say anything to the others because Liz would have been scared.'

'What did you see?'

'I saw snakes.'

'No!'

'Yes, I did. And they're all turned to stone. They curled along the floor, and I kicked one and it was hard like one of those stone fish they found above Bottom.'

'Well,' Number Three said, 'that seems to prove it,' and they were silent again, weighed down by the magnitude of their discovery. Above their heads, between them and the great chimney, rose yet another house in this nest of houses, and a ladder went up to it from a spot close to where they stood. On the front of the house twenty feet up was a meaningless design in tarnished yellow. Pete memorized the shape, to draw it later in the dust for his father who would never, he knew, believe their story, who would think they had dug the forfeits – their only proof – up in the ruins at the edge of Bottom. The design was like this:

$$\ulcorner \urcorner \digamma \Lambda \frown \sqsubset$$

'Perhaps that's where Noh lived,' Number Three whispered, gazing at the design as if it contained a clue to the time of legends, and without another word they both began to climb the ladder, just as the other children came on to the roof below them.

'Where are you going?' Liz called, but they didn't bother to answer her. The thick yellow rust came off on their hands as they climbed and climbed.

The other children came chattering up the stairs and then they saw the man too and were silent.

'Noh,' Pete said.

'A giant,' Liz said.

He was a white clean skeleton, and his skull had rolled on to the shoulder-bone and rested there as though it had been laid on a shelf. All round him lay forfeits brighter and thicker than the forfeits in the hall, and the leaves had drifted against the skeleton, so that they had the impression that he was lying stretched in sleep in a green field. A shred of faded blue material, which the birds had somehow neglected to take at nesting-time, still lay, as though for modesty, across the loins, but when Liz took it up in her fingers it crumbled away to a little powder. Number Three paced the length of the skeleton. He said, 'He was nearly six feet tall.'

'So there *were* giants,' Liz said.

'And they played forfeits,' Number Two said, as though that reassured him of their human nature.

'Moon ought to see him,' Number One said; 'that would take him down a peg.' Moon was the tallest man ever known in Bottom, but he was more than a foot shorter than this length of white bone. They stood around the skeleton with eyes lowered as though they were ashamed of something.

At last Number Two said suddenly, 'It's late. I'm going home,' and he made his hop-and-skip way to the ladder, and after a moment's hesitation Number One and Number Three limped after him. A forfeit went crunch under a foot. No one had picked these forfeits up, nor any other of the strange objects which lay gleaming among the leaves. Nothing here was treasure-trove; everything belonged to the dead giant.

At the top of the ladder Pete turned to see what Liz was up to. She sat squatting on the thigh-bones of the skeleton, her naked buttocks rocking to and fro as though in the act of possession. When he went back to her he found that she was weeping.

'What is it, Liz?' he asked.

She leaned forward towards the gaping mouth. 'He's beauti-ful,' she said, 'he's so beautiful. And he's a giant. Why aren't there giants now?' She began to keen over him like a little old woman at a funeral. 'He's six feet tall,' she cried, exagger-ating a little, 'and he has beautiful straight legs. No one has straight legs in Bottom. Why aren't there giants now? Look at his lovely mouth with all the teeth. Who has teeth like that in Bottom?'

'*You* are pretty, Liz,' Pete said, shuffling around in front of her, trying in vain to straighten his own spine like the skele-ton's, beseeching her to notice him, feeling jealousy for those straight white bones upon the floor and for the first time a sensation of love for the little bandy-legged creature bucketing to and fro.

'Why aren't there any giants now?' she repeated for the third time, with her tears falling among the bird-droppings. He went sadly to the window and looked out. Below him the red rock split the floor, and up the long slope of the roof he could see the three children scrambling towards the cliff; awkward, with short uneven limbs, they moved like little crabs. He looked down at his own stunted and uneven legs and heard her begin to keen again for a whole world lost.

'He's six feet tall and he has beautiful straight legs.'